david levithan

ALFRED A. KNOPF NEW YORK

THIS IS A BORZOI BOOK PUBLISHED BY ALFRED A. KNOPF

Copyright © 2003 by David Levithan

All rights reserved under International and Pan-American Copyright Conventions. Published in the United States by Alfred A. Knopf, an imprint of Random House Children's Books, a division of Random House, Inc., New York, and simultaneously in Canada by Random House of Canada Limited, Toronto. Distributed by Random House, Inc., New York. KNOPF, BORZOI BOOKS, and the colophon are registered trademarks of Random House, Inc.

www.randomhouse.com/teens

Library of Congress Cataloging-in-Publication Data
Levithan, David.
Boy meets boy / by David Levithan.
p. cm.

ISBN 0-375-82400-6 (trade) — ISBN 0-375-92400-0 (lib. bdg.)
[1. Teenage boys—Fiction. 2. Gay teenagers—Fiction. 3. Male friendship—Fiction.]
I. Title.
PS3562.E922175 B69 2003
813'.54—dc21
2002073154

Printed in the United States of America
September 2003
10 9 8 7 6 5
First Edition

for Tony
(even if he only exists in a song)

Acknowledgments

This book started out as a story I wrote for my friends for Valentine's Day. First and foremost, it still belongs to them. You should all know who you are, and how much you mean to me.

I want to thank the following people who inspired and encouraged me (either knowingly or not) as I wrote this story: Mike Rothman, Nancy Mercado, Eliza Sporn, Shira Epstein, Christopher Olenzak, Bethany Buck, Janet Vultee, Ann Martin, John Heginbotham, Edric Mesmer, and Rodney Bender. I am also indebted to all the writers, editors, and production editors with whom I have worked, from the BSC to PUSH. The source of this book's dedication is the song "Tony" by Patty Griffin; whenever I needed motivation, all I had to do was press play and there it was.

I owe Shana Corey, Brian Selznick, and David Serlin for the pivotal moment that led to this story becoming this book. I am also very happy that Chris Krovatin came into my life while I was finishing it.

All the umbrellas in London couldn't stop me from showering my editor, Nancy Hinkel, with praise.

Billy Merrell brings me joy.

My deepest thanks go to my family and to my friends who are family. Cary Retlin, David Leventhal, and Jennifer Bodner mean the world to me. And I am proud to be the intersection of my brother Adam, my niece Paige, and all the Levithans, Golbers, Streiters, and Allens I know and love. My parents are, quite simply, the best.

Thank you all.

Now away we go

9 P.M. on a November Saturday. Joni, Tony, and I are out on the town. Tony is from the next town over and he needs to get out. His parents are extremely religious. It doesn't even matter which religion—they're all the same at a certain point, and few of them want a gay boy cruising around with his friends on a Saturday night. So every week Tony feeds us bible stories, then on Saturday we show up at his doorstep well versed in parables and earnestness, dazzling his parents with our blinding purity. They slip him a twenty and tell him to enjoy our study group. We go spend the money on romantic comedies, dimestore toys, and diner jukeboxes. Our happiness is the closest we'll ever come to a generous God, so we figure Tony's parents would understand, if only they weren't set on misunderstanding so many things.

Tony has to be home by midnight, so we are on a Cinderella mission. With this in mind, we keep our eye on the ball.

There isn't really a gay scene or a straight scene in our town. They got all mixed up a while back, which I think is for the best. Back when I was in second grade, the older gay kids who didn't flee to the city for entertainment would have to make their own fun. Now it's all good. Most of the straight guys try to sneak into the Queer Beer bar. Boys who love boys flirt with girls who love girls. And whether your heart is strictly ballroom or bluegrass punk, the dance floors are open to whatever you have to offer.

This is my town. I've lived here all my life.

Tonight, our Gaystafarian bud Zeke is gigging at the local chain bookstore. Joni has a driver's license from the state where her grandmother lives, so she drives us around in the family sedan. We roll down the windows and crank the radio — we like the idea of our music spilling out over the whole neighborhood, becoming part of the air. Tony has a desperate look tonight, so we let him control the dial. He switches to a Mope Folk station, and we ask him what's going on.

"I can't say," he tells us, and we know what he means. That nameless empty.

We try to cheer him up by treating him to a blue Slurp-Slurp at the local 24-7. We each take sips, to see whose tongue can get the bluest. Once Tony's sticking his tongue out with the rest of us, we know he's going to be okay.

Zeke's already jamming by the time we get to the highway bookstore. He's put his stage in the European History section, and every now and then he'll throw names like Hadrian and Copernicus into his mojo rap. The place is crowded. A little girl in the children's section puts the Velveteen Rabbit on her shoulders for a better view. Her moms are standing behind her, holding hands and nodding to Zeke's tune. The Gaystafarian crowd has planted itself in the Gardening section, while the three straight members of the guys' lacrosse team are ogling a bookstore clerk from Literature. She doesn't seem to mind. Her glasses are the color of licorice.

I move through the crowd with ease, sharing nods and smiling hellos. I love this scene, this floating reality. I am a solo flier looking out over the land of Boyfriends and Girlfriends. I am three notes in the middle of a song.

Joni grabs me and Tony, pulling us into Self-Help. There are a few monkish types already there, some of them trying to ignore the music and learn the Thirteen Ways to Be an Effective Person. I know Joni's brought us here because sometimes you just have to dance like a madman in the Self-Help section of your local bookstore. So we dance. Tony hesitates—he isn't much of a dancer. But as I've told him a million times, when it comes to true dancing, it doesn't matter what you look like—it's all about the joy you feel.

Zeke's jive is infectious. People are crooning and swooning into one another. You can see the books on the shelves in kaleidoscope form—spinning rows of colors, the passing blur of words.

I sway. I sing. I elevate. My friends are by my side, and Zeke is working the Huguenots into his melody. I spin around and knock a few books off the shelves. When the song is through, I bend to pick them up.

I grasp on the ground and come face to face with a cool pair of sneakers.

"This yours?" a voice above the sneakers asks.

I look up. And there he is.

His hair points in ten different directions. His eyes are a little close together, but man, are they green. There's a little birthmark on his neck, the shape of a comma.

I think he's wonderful.

He's holding a book out to me. *Migraines Are Only in Your Mind.*

I am aware of my breathing. I am aware of my heartbeat. I am aware that my shirt is half untucked. I take the book from him and say thanks. I put it back on the shelf. There's no way that Self-Help can help me now.

"Do you know Zeke?" I ask, nodding to the stand.

"No," the boy answers. "I just came for a book."

"I'm Paul."

"I'm Noah."

He shakes my hand. I am touching his hand.

I can feel Joni and Tony keeping their curious distance.

"Do *you* know Zeke?" Noah asks. "His tunes are magnificent."

I roll the word in my head—*magnificent*. It's like a gift to hear.

"Yeah, we go to school together," I say casually.

"The high school?"

"That's the one." I'm looking down. He has perfect hands.

"I go there, too."

"You do?" I can't believe I've never seen him before. If I'd seen him before, it would have damn well registered.

"Two weeks now. Are you a senior?"

I look down at my Keds. "I'm a sophomore."

"Cool."

Now I fear he's humoring me. There's nothing cool about being a sophomore. Even a new kid would know that.

"Noah?" another voice interrupts, insistent and expectant. A girl has appeared behind him. She is dressed in a lethal combination of pastels. She's young, but she looks like she could be a hostess on the Pillow and Sofa Network.

"My sister," he explains, much to my relief. She trudges off. It is clear that he is supposed to follow.

We hover for a second. Our momentary outro of regret. Then he says, "I'll see you around."

I want to say *I hope so,* but suddenly I'm afraid of being too forward. I can flirt with the best of them—but only when it doesn't matter.

This suddenly matters.

"See you," I echo. He leaves as Zeke begins another set. When he gets to the door, he turns to look at me and smiles. I feel myself blush and bloom.

Now I can't dance. It's hard to groove when you've got things on your mind. Sometimes you can use the dancing to fight them off.

But I don't want to fight this off.

I want to keep it.

"So do you think he's on the bride's side or the groom's side?" Joni asks after the gig.

"I think people can sit wherever they want nowadays," I reply.

Zeke is packing up his gear. We're leaning against the front of his VW bus, squinting so we can turn the streetlamps into stars.

"I think he likes you," Joni says.

"Joni," I protest, "you thought *Wes Travers* liked me—and all he wanted to do was copy my homework."

"This is different. He was in Art and Architecture the whole time Zeke was playing. Then you caught his eye and he ambled over. It wasn't Self-Help he was after."

I look at my watch. "It's almost pumpkin time. Where's Tony?"

We find him a little ways over, lying in the middle of the street, on an island that's been adopted by the local Kiwanis Club.

His eyes are closed. He is listening to the music of the traffic going by.

I climb over the divider and tell him study group's almost over.

"I know," he says to the sky. Then, as he's getting up, he adds, "I like it here."

I want to ask him, *Where is here?* Is it this island, this town, this world? More than anything in this strange life, I want Tony to be happy. We found out a long time ago that we weren't meant to fall in love with each other. But a part of me still fell in hope with him. I want a fair world. And in a fair world, Tony would shine.

I could tell him this, but he wouldn't accept it. He would leave it on the island instead of folding it up and keeping it with him, just to know it was there.

We all need a place. I have mine—this topsy-turvy collection of friends, tunes, afterschool activities, and dreams. I want him to have a place, too. When he says "I like it here," I don't want there to be a sad undertone. I want to be able to say, *So stay*.

But I remain quiet, because now it's a quiet night, and Tony is already walking back to the parking lot.

"What's a Kiwanis?" he yells over his shoulder.

I tell him it sounds like a bird. A bird from somewhere far, far away.

"Hey Gay Boy. Hey Tony. Hey folkie chick."

I don't even need to look up from the pavement. "Hello, Ted," I say.

He's walked up just as we're about to drive out. I can hear Tony's parents miles away, finishing up their evening prayers. They will expect us soon. Ted's car is blocking us in. Not out of spite. Out of pure obliviousness. He is a master of obliviousness.

"You're in our way," Joni points out from the driver's seat. Her irritation is quarter-hearted, at best.

"You look nice tonight," he replies.

Ted and Joni have broken up twelve times in the past few years. Which means they've gotten back together eleven times. I always feel we're teetering on the precipice of Reunion Number Twelve.

Ted is smart and good-looking, but he doesn't use it to good effect, like a rich person who never gives to charity. His world rarely expands farther than the nearest mirror. Even in tenth grade, he likes to think of himself as the king of our school. He hasn't stopped to notice it's a democracy.

The problem with Ted is that he's not a total loss. Sometimes, from the murk of his self-notice, he will make a crystal-clear comment that's so insightful you wish you'd made it yourself. A little of that can go a long way. Especially with Joni.

"Really," she says now, her voice easier, "we've gotta go."

"You've run out of chapter and verse for your study group? 'O

Lord, as I walk through the valley of the shadow of doubt, at least let me wear a Walkman....' "

"The Lord is my DJ," Tony says solemnly. "I shall not want."

"One day, Tony—I swear we'll free you." Ted bangs the hood of the car to emphasize the point, and Tony gives him a salute. Ted moves his car, and we're off again.

Joni's clock says it's 12:48, but we're okay, since it's been an hour fast since Daylight Saving Time ended. We drive into the blue-black, the radio mellow now, the hour slowly turning from nighttime to sleep.

Noah is a hazy memory in my mind. I am losing track of the way he ran my nerves; the giddiness is now diffusing in the languid air, becoming a mysterious blur of good feeling.

"How come I've never seen him before?" I ask.

"Maybe you were just waiting for the right time to notice," Tony says.

Maybe he's right.

Paul is Gay

I've always known I was gay, but it wasn't confirmed until I was in kindergarten.

It was my teacher who said so. It was right there on my kindergarten report card: PAUL IS DEFINITELY GAY AND HAS VERY GOOD SENSE OF SELF.

I saw it on her desk one day before naptime. And I have to admit: I might not have realized I was different if Mrs. Benchly hadn't pointed it out. I mean, I was five years old. I just *assumed* boys were attracted to other boys. Why else would they spend all of their time together, playing on teams and making fun of the girls? I assumed it was because we all liked each other. I was still unclear how girls fit into the picture, but I thought I knew the boy thing A-OK.

Imagine my surprise to find out that I wasn't entirely right. Imagine my surprise when I went through all the other reports and found out that not one of the other boys had been labeled DEFINITELY GAY. (In all fairness, none of the others had a VERY GOOD SENSE OF SELF, either.) Mrs. Benchly caught me at her desk and looked quite alarmed. Since I was more than a little confused, I asked her for some clarification.

"Am I definitely gay?" I asked.

Mrs. Benchly looked me over and nodded.

"What's gay?" I asked.

"It's when a boy likes other boys," she explained.

I pointed over to the painting corner, where Greg Easton was wrestling on the ground with Ted Halpern.

"Is Greg gay?" I asked.

"No," Mrs. Benchly answered. "At least, not yet."

Interesting. I found it all very interesting.

Mrs. Benchly explained a little more to me—the whole boys-liking-girls thing. I can't say I understood. Mrs. Benchly asked me if I'd noticed that marriages were mostly made up of men and women. I had never really thought of marriages as things that involved liking. I had just assumed this man-woman arrangement was yet another adult quirk, like flossing. Now Mrs. Benchly was telling me something much bigger. Some sort of silly global conspiracy.

"But that's not how I feel," I protested. My attention was a little distracted because Ted was now pulling up Greg Easton's shirt, and that was kind of cool. "How I feel is what's right . . . right?"

"For you, yes," Mrs. Benchly told me. "What you feel is absolutely right for you. Always remember that."

And I have. Sort of.

That night, I held my big news until after my favorite Nickelodeon block was over. My father was in the kitchen, doing dishes. My mother was in the den with me, reading on the couch. Quietly, I walked over to her.

"GUESS WHAT!" I said. She jumped, then tried to pretend she hadn't been surprised. Since she didn't close her book—she only marked the page with her finger—I knew I didn't have much time.

"What?" she asked.

"I'm gay!"

Parents never react the way you want them to. I thought, at the

9

very least, my mother would take her finger out of the book. But no. Instead she turned in the direction of the kitchen and yelled to my father.

"Honey . . . Paul's learned a new word!"

It took my parents a couple of years. But eventually they got used to it.

Besides my parents, Joni was the first person I ever came out to.

This was in second grade.

We were under my bed at the time. We were under my bed because Joni had come over to play, and under my bed was easily the coolest place in the whole house. We had brought flashlights and were telling ghost stories as a lawn mower grrrrred outside. We pretended it was the Grim Reaper. We were playing our favorite game: Avoid Death.

"So a poisonous snake has just bitten your left arm—what do you do?" Joni asked.

"I try to suck the poison out."

"But that doesn't work. It's spreading up your arm. . . ."

"So I take my axe and chop off my arm."

"But once you chop off your arm, you're bleeding to death."

"So I pull off my shirt and tie it around the stump to stop the blood."

"But a vulture smells the blood and comes swooping down at you."

"So I use my right arm to pick up the left arm that I cut off, and I use it to bat the vulture away!"

"But . . ."

Joni trailed off. At first, I figured I had her stumped. Then she leaned over, her eyelids closing. She smelled like bubblegum and bicycle grease. Before I knew it, her lips were coming near mine. I was so freaked out, I stood up. Since we were still under my bed, I crashed into the bottom of my mattress.

Her eyes opened quickly after that.

"What'd you do that for?" we both yelled at the same time.

"Don't you like me?" Joni asked, clearly hurt.

"Yeah," I said. "But, you know, I'm gay."

"Oh. Cool. Sorry."

"No problem."

There was a pause, and then Joni continued.

"But the vulture pulls your left arm out of your hand and begins to hit you with it. . . ."

At that moment I knew Joni and I were going to be friends for a good long time.

It was with Joni's help that I became the first openly gay class president in the history of Ms. Farquar's third-grade class.

Joni was my campaign manager. She was the person who came up with my campaign slogan: VOTE FOR ME . . . I'M GAY!

I thought it rather oversimplified my stance on the issues (pro-recess, anti-gym), but Joni said it was sure to generate media attention. At first, she wanted the slogan to be VOTE FOR ME . . . I'M A GAY, but I pointed out that this could easily be misread as VOTE FOR ME . . . I'M A GUY, which would certainly lose me votes. So the A was struck, and the race began in earnest.

My biggest opponent was (I'm sorry to say) Ted Halpern. His first slogan was VOTE FOR ME . . . I'M NOT GAY, which only made him seem dull. Then he tried YOU CAN'T VOTE FOR HIM . . . HE'S GAY, which was pretty stupid, because nobody likes to be told who they can (or can't) vote for. Finally, in the days leading up to the election, he resorted to DONT VOTE FOR THE FAG. Hello? Joni threatened to beat him up, but I knew he'd played right into our hands. When the election was held, he was left with the rather tiny lint-head vote, while I carried the girl vote, the open-minded guy vote, the third-grade closet-case vote, and the Ted-hater vote. It was a total blowout, and when it was all over, Joni beat Ted up anyway.

The next day at lunch, Cody O'Brien traded me two Twinkies for a box of raisins—clearly an unequal trade. The next day, I gave him three Yodels for a Fig Newton.

This was my first flirtation.

Cody was my date for my fifth-grade semi-formal. Or at least he was supposed to be my date. Two days before the big shindig, we had a fight over a Nintendo cartridge he'd borrowed from me and lost. I know it's a small thing to break up over, but really, the way he handled it (lying! deceit!) was symptomatic of bigger problems. Luckily, we parted on friendly terms. Joni was supposed to be my back-up date, but she surprised me by saying she was going with Ted. She swore to me he'd changed.

This was also symptomatic of bigger problems. But there was no way of knowing it then.

In sixth grade, Cody, Joni, a lesbian fourth grader named Laura, and I formed our elementary school's first gay-straight alliance. Quite honestly, we took one look around and figured the straight kids needed our help. For one thing, they were all wearing the same clothes. Also (and this was critical), they couldn't dance to save their lives. Our semi-formal dance floor could have easily been mistaken for a coop of pre-Thanksgiving turkeys. This was not acceptable.

Luckily, our principal was cooperative, and allowed us to play a minute or two of "I Will Survive" and "Bizarre Love Triangle" after the Pledge of Allegiance was read each morning. Membership in the gay-straight alliance soon surpassed that of the football team (which isn't to say there wasn't overlap). Ted refused to join, but he couldn't stop Joni from signing them up for swing dance classes twice a week at recess.

Since I was unattached at the time, and since I was starting to feel that I had met everyone there was to meet at our elementary school, I would often sneak out with Laura to the AV room, where we'd watch Audrey Hepburn movies until the recess bell would ring, and reality would beckon once more.

In eighth grade, I was tackled by two high school wrestlers after a late-night showing of *Priscilla, Queen of the Desert* at our local theater. At first, I thought it was a strange kind of foreplay, but then I realized that their grunts were actually insults—queer, faggot, the usual. I wasn't about to take such verbal abuse from strangers—only Joni was allowed to speak to me that way. Luckily, I had gone to the movies with a bunch of my friends from the fencing team, so they just pulled out their foils and disarmed the lugheads. (One of them, I've since heard, is now a drag queen in Columbus, Ohio. I like to think I had something to do with that.)

I was learning that notoriety came with a certain backlash. I had to be careful. I had a gay food column in the local paper—"Dining OUT"—which was a modest success. I'd declined numerous pleas to run for student council president, because I knew it would interfere with my direction of the school musical (I won't bore you with the details, but let me just say that Cody O'Brien was an Auntie Mame for the ages).

All in all, life through junior high was pretty fun. I didn't really have a life that was so much out of the ordinary. The usual series of crushes, confusions, and intensities.

Then I meet Noah and things become complicated. I sense it immediately, driving home from Zeke's gig. I suddenly feel more complicated.

Not bad complicated.

Just complicated.

The Homecoming
Queen's Dilemma

I look for him in the hallways on Monday. I hope that he's looking for me, too.

Joni promises me she'll be my search party spy. I'm afraid she'll get too carried away with the job, dragging Noah over to me by the ear if she finds him.

But the connection isn't made. No matter how far I drift from the hallway conversations I'm having, I never drift into him. The halls are awash in Homecoming Pride posters and post-weekend gossip. Everybody is jingling and jangling; I look for Noah like I'd look for a pocket of calm.

Instead I run into Infinite Darlene. Or, more accurately, she runs on over to me. There are few sights grander at eight in the morning than a six-foot-four football player scuttling through the halls in high heels, a red shock wig, and more-than-passable make-up. If I wasn't so used to it, I might be taken aback.

"Ah'm so glad I caught you," Infinite Darlene exclaims, sounding like Scarlett O'Hara as played by Clark Gable. "Things are such a mess!"

I don't know when Infinite Darlene and I first became friends. Perhaps it was back when she was still Daryl Heisenberg, but that's not very likely; few of us can remember what Daryl Heisenberg was like, since Infinite Darlene consumed him so completely. He was a decent football player, but nowhere near as good as when he started wearing false eyelashes.

Infinite Darlene doesn't have it easy. Being both star quarterback and homecoming queen has its conflicts. And sometimes it's hard for her to fit in. The other drag queens in our school rarely sit with her at lunch; they say she doesn't take good enough care of her nails, and that she looks a little too buff in a tank top. The football players are a little more accepting, although there was a spot of trouble a year ago when Chuck, the second-string quarterback, fell in love with her and got depressed when she said he wasn't her type.

I am not alarmed when Infinite Darlene tells me things are *such a mess.* For Infinite Darlene, things are always *such a mess;* if they weren't, she wouldn't have nearly enough to talk about.

This time, though, it's a real dilemma.

"Coach Ginsburg is going to have my hat," she declares. "It's the frickin' Homecoming Pride rally this afternoon. He wants me to march with the rest of the team. But as homecoming queen, I'm also supposed to be *introducing* the team. If I don't do the proper introductions, my tiara might be in doubt. Trilby Pope would take my place, which would be ghastly, ghastly, ghastly. Her boobs are faker than mine."

"You think Trilby Pope would stoop that low?" I ask.

"Is the Pope shrewish? *Of course* she would stoop that low. And she'd have gravity problems getting back up."

Usually Infinite Darlene acts like she's in a perpetual congeniality contest. But Trilby Pope is her weak spot. They used to be good friends, able to recount an hour's worth of activity with three hours' worth of conversation. Then Trilby fell into the field hockey crowd. She tried to convince Infinite Darlene to join her, but football was the same season. They drifted into different practices and different groups of friends. Trilby started to wear a lot of plaid, which Infinite

Darlene despised. She started to hang with rugby boys. It all became very fraught. Finally, they had a friendship break-up—an exchange of heated classroom notes, folded in the shape of artillery. They averted their glances dramatically when they passed in the halls. Trilby still has some of Infinite Darlene's accessories, from when they used to swap. Infinite Darlene tells everybody (except Trilby) that she wants them back.

My attention is beginning to wander from the conversation. I am still scanning the hallways for Noah, knowing full well that if I see him, I will most probably duck into the nearest doorway, blushing furiously.

"I do declare," Infinite Darlene does declare, "*what* has gotten you so distracted?"

It is here that I feel the limit of our friendship. Because while Infinite Darlene feels comfortable telling me everything, I am afraid that if I tell her something, it will no longer be mine. It will belong to the whole school.

"I'm just looking for someone," I hedge.

"Aren't we all?" Infinite Darlene vamps ruefully. I think I'm off the hook, but then she adds, "Is it someone *special*?"

"It's nothing," I say, crossing my fingers. I pray that it's not nothing. Yes, I pray to my Big Lesbian God Who Doesn't Really Exist. I say to her: *I don't ask for much. I swear. But I would really love Noah to be everything I hope he'll be. Please let him be someone I can groove with, and who wants to groove with me.*

My denial has sent Infinite Darlene back to her own dilemma. I tell her she should march with the football team while wearing her homecoming queen regalia. It seems like a good compromise to me.

Infinite Darlene starts to nod. Then her eyes see something over my shoulder and flash anger.

"Don't look now," she whispers.

Of course, I turn and look. And there's Kyle Kimball walking by.

Turning away from me like he might catch plague from a single bubonic glance.

Kyle is the only straight boy I've ever kissed. (He didn't realize he was straight at the time.) We went out for a few weeks last year, in ninth grade. He is the only ex I'm not on speaking terms with. Sometimes I even feel like he hates me. It's a very strange feeling. I'm not used to being hated.

"He'll learn," Infinite Darlene says as Kyle recedes into a classroom. She's been saying that for a year now, without ever telling me who Kyle's going to learn from. I still wonder if it's supposed to be me.

With some break-ups, all you can think about afterwards is how badly it ended and how much the other person hurt you. With others, you become sentimental for the good times and lose track of what went wrong. When I think of Kyle, the beginnings and the endings are all mixed up. I see his enraptured face reflected in the light of a flickering movie screen; passing him a note and having him rip it into confetti-sized pieces without reading it; his hand taking mine for the first time, on the way to math class; him calling me a liar and a loser; the first time I knew he liked me, when I caught him hovering around my locker before I actually got there; the first time I knew he didn't like me anymore, when I went to give him back a book I'd borrowed and he pulled away instinctively.

He said I'd tricked him. He said it to everyone.

Only a few people believed him. But it wasn't what they thought that mattered to me. It was what he thought. And if he really believed it.

"He's the worst," Infinite Darlene says. But even she knows this isn't true. He is far from the worst.

Seeing Kyle always takes some of the volume out of my soundtrack. Now I'm no longer floating on a Noah high.

Infinite Darlene tries to cheer me up.

"I have chocolate," she says, reaching a big hand into her purse for a Milky Way mini.

I am sucking at the caramel and nougat when Joni comes up to us with her latest Noah Report. Sadly, it's the same as the last five.

"I haven't been able to find him," she says. "I've found people who know who he is, but nobody seems to know *where* he is. Chuck was helping me before, and Chuck said that he's one of those arty types. Now, from Chuck that wasn't an ultimate compliment, but at least it pointed me in the right direction. I looked at the wall outside the art room and found a photo he did. Chuck helped me get it."

I am not really alarmed by Joni's thievery—we take things off walls and put them back all the time. But my inner security device does take notice of the number of times that Joni's name-checked Chuck. In the past, I've been able to tell that things with Ted were getting better when Joni began to name-check him again. The fact that it's now Chuck has looped me for a throw.

Joni takes a small, framed photograph out of her bag. The frame is the color of Buddy Holly's glasses, and has largely the same effect.

"You have to look at it closely," Joni tells me.

I hold the photo up to my face, ignoring my own reflection to see what lies beneath. At first I see the man in the chair, toward the back of the photo. He's the age of my grandfather and is sitting in an old wooden rocker, laughing his head off. Then I realize he's sitting in a room covered by snow globes. There must be hundreds—maybe thousands—of the small plastic shakers, each with its own blurry locale. Snow globes cover the floor, the counters, the shelves, the table at the man's arm.

It's a very cool photograph.

"You can't keep it," Joni says.

"I know, I know." I look at it for a minute more, then hand it back.

Infinite Darlene has kept quiet through this whole exchange. But she's about to burst with curiosity.

"He's just some guy," I say.

"Do tell," she insists.

So I do. Tell.

And I know as I do that he isn't "just some guy." There was something in our two minutes together that felt like it could last for years. Telling Infinite Darlene this doesn't just feel like I'm setting myself up for gossip.

No, it feels like I'm putting my whole heart on the line.

Pride and Joy

Joni, Ted, and I sit together for the Homecoming Pride Rally that afternoon. It's the first rally that I've ever been in the stands for. This is due to a fluke of scheduling. Our school has too many activities and teams to be represented in each and every cheering session, so whenever we have a rally, only a dozen groups are spotlighted. They'd asked me to bring my acting troupe this time around, but I felt such recognition might damage our art—putting the personality before the performance, as it were. So as a result I am sitting in the bleachers of our gymnasium, trying to gauge the Joni-and-Ted barometer. Right now, it looks like the pressure is high. Ted keeps looking over at Joni, but Joni isn't looking as much at Ted.

He turns to me instead.

"You find your boyfriend yet?" he asks.

Panicked, I look around to see if Noah is in the immediate vicinity. Luckily, he is not.

I am starting to wonder if he actually exists.

The principal's secretary gets up to the microphone to start the rally. Everybody knows that she wields the real power in the school, so it makes sense to have her leading things here.

The gymnasium doors open and the cheerleaders come riding in on their Harleys. The crowd goes wild.

We are, I believe, the only high school in America with a biker cheerleading team. But I could be wrong. A few years ago, it was decided that having a posse of motorcycles gun around the fields and courts was a much bigger cheer-inducer than any pom-pom routine could ever hope to be. Now, in an intricately choreographed display, the Harleys swerve around the gym, starting off in a pyramid the shape of a bird migration, then splitting up into spins and corners. For a finale, the cheerleaders rev all at once and shoot themselves off a ramp emblazoned with our high school's name. They are rewarded with massive applause.

Already the rally is doing its job. I am proud to be a student at my high school.

The tennis team is the next up. My brother and his friend Mara are the doubles champions, so they get a pretty good reception. I try to cheer loudly so Jay can hear my voice above the crowd. He's a senior now, and I know he's started to feel sad about everything coming to an end. Next year, he'll be on a college tennis team. It won't be the same.

After the tennis team has been cheered, our school cover band comes out to play. The cover band's stats are actually better than the tennis team's—at this past year's Dave Matthews Cover Band Competition, they went all the way to the finals with their cover of the Dave Matthews Band covering "All Along the Watchtower," only to be defeated by a cover band that played "Typical Situation" while standing on their heads. Now they launch into a cover of "One Day More" from *Les Misérables,* and I admire the lead singer's versatility.

After an encore of Depeche Mode's "Personal Jesus," the principal's secretary asks for quiet and introduces this year's homecoming king and queen. Infinite Darlene strides out in a pink ball gown, covered in part by her quarterback jersey. The homecoming king, Dave Sprat, hangs from her arm, a good thirteen inches shorter than her (if you count the heels).

Infinite Darlene is holding a portable microphone we borrowed from Zeke's van, so she can introduce and march at the same time. As the school cover band strikes up a skacore version of "We Are the Champions" (we're not *entirely* without tradition), the members of the football team line up for their presentation.

I lean over to Joni. She's fixing her eyes on Chuck.

I honestly don't know why. Chuck is the second-string quarterback who fell for Infinite Darlene and got all upset when she didn't return his affections. He was real bitter about it, worse than Ted in his fouler moods. Ted, at least, is able to lose his cool without totally losing his sense of humor. I'm not sure that Chuck's the same way. I wish Tony went to our school, so I could lift my eyebrow and get his take on the situation.

Ted doesn't seem to notice where Joni's glance is taking her. He is looking elsewhere.

"Is that him?" he asks.

Because he's Ted, he goes right ahead and points at someone in the stands across the gymnasium. I squint to make out the faces from the crowd. At first, I think he's pointing at Kyle, who is somewhat subdued in his applause for the football players as Infinite Darlene introduces them. Then I realize Ted is pointing a few rows up.

I see an empty seat. Then, next to it, I see Noah.

He senses me looking. I swear. He looks right at me.

Or maybe he's looking at Ted, who's still pointing.

"Put your finger down," I say between gritted teeth.

"Chill," Ted tells me, moving his finger through the air, as if he hadn't been pointing at Noah at all. I try to play along.

When the whole pointing charade is over, I see that Noah's still where he was a second ago. I don't know why I thought he would have disappeared. I guess I don't believe these things can ever be easy, although I also don't see why they have to be hard.

Joni's broken her attention from Chuck for long enough to get what's going on.

"Don't just sit here," she says.

"If you don't go over there, I will—and I'll tell him all about your crush," Ted informs me. I'm not sure if he's kidding or not.

It's a mighty thin border between peer pressure and bravery. Knowing that Joni and Ted aren't going to let me get out of it, I head to Noah's side of the gym. One of the teachers shoots me a stay-in-your-seat glance, but I wave her off. Over the loudspeakers, I can hear Infinite Darlene's crystal voice: "And now, introducing the quarterback ... the one ... the only ... *ME*!"

I look at the crowd. Everyone cheers, except for some of the more elitist drag queens, who feign disinterest.

I duck behind the bleachers, weaving to the stairs. I wonder what I'll say. I wonder if I'm about to make a fool of myself.

All I can feel is this intensity. My mind beating in time with my heart. My steps keeping sway with my hopes.

I get to the bottom of the stands. I've lost track of the space. I can't find Noah. I look back to Joni and Ted. Much to my mortification, they both point me on my way. The football presentation is over and the quiz bowling team is preparing to enter. Infinite Darlene is basking in her last round of applause. I swear she winks when she looks my way.

I focus on the seat next to Noah. I do not focus on his crazy-cool hair, or his blue suede shoes, or the specks of paint on his hands and his arms.

I am beside him.

"Is this seat taken?" I ask.

He looks up at me. And then, after a beat, he breaks out smiling.

"Hey," he says, "I've been looking all over for you."

I don't know what to say. I am so happy and so scared.

There is a roar through the stands as the quiz bowling team is announced. They come sprinting onto the court, rolling for pins while answering questions about Einstein's theory of relativity.

"I've been looking for you, too," I say at last.

He says, "Cool," and it's cool. So cool.

I sit down next to him as the audience cheers for the captain of the quiz bowling team, who's just scored a strike while listing the complete works of the Brontë sisters.

I don't want to scare him by telling him all the things that are scaring me. I don't want him to know how important this is. He has to feel the importance for himself.

So I say, "Those are cool shoes," and we talk about blue suede shoes and the duds store where he shops. We talk as the badminton team lets its birdies fly. We talk as the French Cuisine Club rises the perfect soufflé. We laugh when it falls.

I am looking for signs that he understands me. I am looking for my hopes to be confirmed.

"This is such serendipity, isn't it?" he asks. I almost fall off my seat. I am a firm believer in serendipity—all the random pieces coming together in one wonderful moment, when suddenly you see what their purpose was all along.

We talk about music and find that we like the same kinds of music. We talk about movies and find that we like the same kinds of movies.

"Do you really exist?" I blurt out.

"Not at all," he says with a smile. "I've known that since I was four."

"What happened when you were four?"

"Well, I had this theory. Although I guess I was too young to know it was a theory. You see, I had this imaginary friend. She followed me everywhere—we had to set a place for her at the table, she and I talked all the time—the whole deal. Then it occurred to me that she wasn't the imaginary friend at all. I figured that *I* was the imaginary friend, and she was the one who was real. It made perfect sense to me. My parents disagreed, but I still secretly feel that I'm right."

"What was her name?" I ask.

"Sarah. Yours?"

"Thom. With an *h*."

"Maybe they're together right now."

"Oh, no. I left Thom in Florida. He never liked to travel."

We are not taking each other too seriously, which is a serious plus. The paint on his hands is not quite purple and not quite blue. There is a speck of just-right red on one of his fingers.

The principal's secretary has the microphone again. The rally is almost over.

"I'm glad you found me," Noah says.

"Me too." I want to float, because it's that simple. He's glad I found him. I'm glad I found him. We are not afraid to say this. I am so used to hints and mixed messages, saying things that might mean what they sort of sound like they mean. Games and contests, roles and rituals, talking in twelve languages at once so the true words won't be so obvious. I am not used to a plainspoken, honest truth.

It pretty much blows me away.

I think Noah recognizes this. He's looking at me with a nifty grin. The other people in our row are standing and jostling now, waiting for us to leave so they can get to the aisle and resume their day. I want time to stop.

Time doesn't stop.

"Two sixty-three," Noah tells me.

"?!???" I reply.

"My locker number," he explains. "I'll see you after school."

Now I don't want time to stop. I want it to fast-forward an hour. Noah has become my *until*.

26

As we leave the gym, I can see Kyle shoot me a look. I don't care. Joni and Ted will no doubt be waiting under the bleachers for the full report.

I can sum it up in one word:

Joy.

Hallway Traffic
(Complications Ensue)

Self-esteem can be so exhausting. I want to cut my hair, change my clothes, erase the pimple from the near-tip of my nose, and strengthen my upper-arm definition, all in the next hour. But I can't do that, because (a) it's impossible, and (b) if I make any of these changes, Noah will notice that I've changed, and I don't want him to know how into him I am.

I hope Mr. B can save me. I pray his physics class today will transfix me in such a way that I will forget about what awaits me at the other end. But as Mr. B bounds around the room with anti-gravitational enthusiasm, I just can't join his parade. *Two sixty-four* has become my new mantra. I roll the number over in my head, hoping it will reveal something to me (other than a locker number). I replay my conversation with Noah, trying to transcribe it into memory since I don't dare write it down in my notebook.

The hour passes. As soon as the bell rings, I bolt out of my seat. I don't know where locker 264 is, but I'm sure as hell going to find out.

I plunge into the congested hallway, weaving through the back-slap reunions and locker lunges. I spot locker 435—I'm in the wrong corridor entirely.

"Paul!" a voice yells. There aren't enough Pauls in my school that

I can assume the yell is for someone else. Reluctantly I turn around and see Lyssa Ling about to pull my sleeve.

I already know what she wants. Lyssa Ling doesn't ever talk to me unless she wants me to be on a committee. She's the head of our school's committee on appointing committees, no doubt because she's so good at it.

"What do you want from me now, Lyssa?" I ask. (She's used to this.)

"The Dowager Dance," she says. "I want you to architect it."

I am more than a little surprised. The Dowager Dance is a big deal at our school, and architecting it would mean being in charge of all the decorations and music.

"I thought Dave Davison was architecting it," I say.

Lyssa sighs. "He was. But then he went all Goth on me."

"Cool."

"No. Not cool. We have to give people the freedom to wear something other than black. So are you in or are you out?"

"Can I have some time to think about it?"

"Sixteen seconds."

I count to seventeen and then say, "I'm in."

Lyssa nods, says something about slipping the budget into my locker tomorrow morning, and walks away.

I know it's going to be a rather elaborate budget. The dance was created thirty or so years ago after a local dowager left a stipulation in her will that every year the high school would throw a lavish dance in her honor. (Apparently she was quite a swinger in her day.) The only thing we have to do is feature her portrait prominently and (this is where it gets a little weird) have at least one senior boy dance with it.

At first I am distracted by theme ideas. Then I remember the reason for my after-school existence and continue heading to locker 264 . . . until I am stopped by my English teacher, who wants to compliment me on my reading of Oscar Wilde in yesterday's class. I can't exactly blow her off, nor can I blow off Infinite Darlene when she asks me how her double role at the Homecoming Pride Rally went.

The minutes are ticking away. I hope Noah is equally delayed, and that we'll arrive at his locker at the same time, one of those wonderful kismet connections that seem like signs of great things to come.

"Hey, Boy Romeo."

Ted is now alongside me, luckily not stopping as he talks.

"Hey," I echo.

"Where you goin'?"

"Locker two sixty-four."

"Isn't that on the second floor?"

I groan. He's right.

We walk up the stairs together.

"Have you seen Joni?" he asks.

Sometimes I feel like fate is dictated by irony (or, at the very least, a rather dark sense of humor). For example, if I am standing next to Joni's on-and-off boyfriend and he says, "Have you seen Joni?" the obvious next step would be to reach the top of the stairway and see Joni in a full frontal embrace with Chuck, on the verge of a serious kiss.

Joni and Chuck don't see us. Their eyes are passionately, expectantly closed. Everybody pauses to look at them. They are a red light in the hallway traffic.

"*Bitch*," Ted whispers, upset. Then he charges back down the stairs.

I know Noah is waiting for me. I know Joni should know what I've seen. I know I don't really like Ted all that much. But more than I know all those things, I know I have to run after Ted to see if he's okay.

He stays a good few paces ahead of me, pushing through hallway after hallway, turn after turn, hitting backpacks off people's shoulders and avoiding the glances of gum-chewing locker waifs. I can't figure out where he's going. Then I realize he doesn't have any particular destination in mind. He's just walking. Walking away.

"Hey, Ted," I call out. We're in a particularly empty corridor, right outside the wood shop.

He turns to me, and there's this conflicted flash in his eyes. The anger wants to drown the shock and the depression.

"Did you know about this?" he asks me.

I shake my head.

"So you don't know how long?"

"No. It's news to me."

"Whatever. I really don't care. She can hook up with whoever she wants. It's not like I was interested. We broke up, you know."

I nod. I wonder if he can actually believe what he's saying. He betrays himself with what he says next.

"I didn't think football players were her type."

I agree, but Ted's not listening to me anymore.

"I gotta go," he says. I want there to be something else for me to say, something to make him feel even marginally better.

I look at my watch. It's been seventeen minutes since the end of school. I use a different stairway to reach the second floor. The locker numbers descend for me: 310 . . . 299 . . . 275 . . .

264.

Nobody home.

I look around for Noah. The halls are nearly deserted now—everyone's either gone home or gone to their activities. The track team races past me on their hallway practice run. I wait another five minutes. A girl I've never seen before, her hair the color of honeydew, walks by and says, "He left about ten minutes ago. He looked disappointed."

I feel like a total loser. I rip a page out of my physics book and write an apology. I go through about five drafts before I'm satisfied that I've managed to sound interested and interesting without seeming entirely daft. All the while, I'm still hoping he'll show up. I slip the note into locker 264.

I head back down to my own locker. Joni is nowhere in sight, which is a good thing. I can't even begin to know what to say to her. I can see why she would have kept the news about Chuck from Ted. But I can't figure out why she never told me. It hurts.

As I slam my locker shut, Kyle walks by me.

He nods and says hi. He even almost smiles.

I am floored.

He keeps walking, not turning back.

My life is crazy, and there's not a single thing I can do about it.

Finding Lost Languages

"Maybe he was saying hi to someone else," I say.

It's a couple of hours later and I'm talking to Tony, recounting the drama to the one person who wasn't there.

"And the smile—well, maybe it was just gas," I add.

Tony nods noncommittally.

"I don't know why Kyle would start talking to me again. It's not like I've done anything differently. And it's not like he's the kind of guy who changes his mind about this kind of thing."

Tony sort of shrugs.

"I wish I could call Noah, but I don't feel like we're close enough for that. I mean, would he even know who I was if I called? Would he recognize my name or my voice? It can wait until tomorrow, right? I don't want to seem too neurotic."

Tony nods again.

"And Joni. What was she thinking, snogging up to Chuck in the middle of the hall like that? Do I let her know that I know, or do I pretend I don't know and secretly count the number of times she talks to me before she lets me know, resenting each and every minute that goes by without her telling me the truth?"

Tony sort of shrugs again.

"Feel free to chime in at any time," I tell him.

"Don't have much to say," he answers with another slight shrug, this one slightly apologetic.

We are at my house, doing each other's homework. We try to do this as often as possible. In much the same way that it's more fun to clean up someone else's room than it is to clean up your own, doing each other's homework is a way to make the homework go faster. Early in our friendship, Tony and I discovered we had similar handwriting. The rest came naturally. Of course, we go to different schools and have different assignments. That's the challenge. And the challenge is what it's all about.

"What book is this paper supposed to be on, anyway?" I ask him.

"Of Mice and Men."

"You mean, 'Please, George, can I pet the bunnies?' "

"Yup."

"Cool, I've read that one."

I start scribbling a topic sentence, while Tony flips through a French-English dictionary to finish my French homework. He takes Spanish.

"You don't seem very surprised about Joni," I say.

"Saw it coming," he replies, not raising his eyes from the dictionary.

"Really? You pictured Ted and me catching them in the hallway?"

"Well, not that part."

"But Chuck?"

"Well, not that part, either. But face it. Joni likes having a boyfriend. And if it's not going to be Ted, it's going to be someone else. If this guy Chuck likes her, odds are she's going to like him back."

"And you approve of this?"

This time he looks right at me. "Who am I to approve or disapprove? If she's happy, then good for her."

There is an unhappy edge in Tony's voice, and it doesn't take many leaps to get to the source of it. Tony's never really had a boyfriend. He's never been in love. I don't exactly know why this is. He's cute, funny, smart, a little gloomy—all attractive qualities. But he still hasn't found what he's looking for. I'm not even sure he knows what that is. Most of the time, he just freezes. He'll have a quiet crush, or even groove with someone who has boyfriend potential . . . and then, before it's even started, it will be over. "It wasn't right," he'll tell us, and that will be that.

This is one of the reasons I don't want to dwell on Noah with him. Although I'm sure he's happy for me, I don't think his happiness for me translates into happiness for himself. I need another way to buoy him. I resort to speaking in a nonexistent language.

"*Hewipso faqua deef?*" I ask him.

"*Tinsin rabblemonk titchticker,*" he replies.

Our record for doing this is six hours, including a lengthy trip to the mall. I don't know how it started—one day we were walking along and I just got tired of speaking English. So I started throwing consonants and vowels together in random arrangements. Without missing a beat, Tony started to speak back to me in the same way. The weird thing is, we've always understood each other. The tone and the gestures say it all.

I first met Tony two years ago, at the Strand in the city. It's one of the best bookstores in the world. We were both looking for a used copy of *The Lost Language of Cranes*. The shelf was eight feet up, so we had to take turns on the ladder. He went first and when he came down with a copy, I asked him if there was another up there. Startled, he told me there was a second copy and even went back up the ladder to get it for me. After he came back down, we hung together for a minute—I asked him if he'd read *Equal Affections* or *A Place I've Never Been,* and he said no, *Lost Language of Cranes* was his first. Then he drifted off to the oversized photography books, while I got lost in fiction.

That would have been it. We would have never known each other, would have never been friends. But that night as I boarded the train home, I saw him sitting alone on a three-seater, already halfway done with the book we'd both bought.

"Book any good?" I asked as I hit the space in the aisle next to him.

At first he didn't realize I was speaking to him. Then he looked up, recognized me, and half smiled.

"It's very good," he answered.

I sat down and we talked some more. I discovered he lived in the next town over from mine. We introduced ourselves. We settled in. I could tell he was nervous, but didn't know why.

A cute guy, a few years older than us, passed through our car. Both of our gazes followed him.

"Damn, he was cute," I said once he'd left.

Tony hesitated for a moment, unsure. Then he smiled.

"Yeah, he was cute." As if he was revealing his deepest secret.

Which, in many ways, he was.

We kept talking. And maybe it was because we were strangers, or maybe it was because we had bought the same book and had thought the same boy was cute. But it was very easy to talk. Riding the train is all about moving forward; our conversation moved like it was on tracks, with no worry of traffic or direction. He told me about his school, which was not like my school, and his parents, who were not like my parents. He didn't use the word *gay* and I didn't need him to. It was understood. This clandestine trip was secret and special to him. He had told his parents he was going on a church retreat. Then he'd hopped on a train to visit the open doors of the open city.

Now the city lights ebbed in their grip over the landscape. The meadowlands waved in the darkness until the smaller cities appeared, then the houses with yards and plastic pools. We had talked our way home, one town apart.

I asked him for his phone number, but he gave me an e-mail address instead. It was safer that way for him. I told him to call me anytime, and we made our next set of plans. In other circumstances, this would have been the start of a romance. But I think we both knew, even then, that what we had was something even more rare, and even more meaningful. I was going to be his friend, and was going to show him possibilities. And he, in turn, would become someone I could trust more than myself.

"Diltaunt aprin zesperado?" Tony asks me now, seeing me lost in thought.

"Gastemicama," I answer decisively.

I'm good.

It's hard for me to concentrate on Tony's homework, with so many things to think about. Somehow I manage to write three pages before my brother comes downstairs and offers to give Tony a ride home. Of all my friends, Jay likes Tony best. I think they have compatible silences. I can imagine them on the way back to Tony's, not saying a word. Jay respects Tony, and I respect Jay for that.

I already know that Tony won't give me any advice about what to do with Noah or Joni or Kyle. It's not that he doesn't care (I'm sure he does). He just likes people to do their own thing.

"Lifstat beyune hegra," he says when departing. But his tone holds no clues. Good-bye? Good luck? Call Noah?

I don't know.

"Yaroun," I reply.

Good-bye. See you tomorrow.

I head back to my room and finish my homework. I don't look over what Tony's already written. I'm sure it's fine.

I spend the rest of the evening in a television daze. For the first time in a long time, I don't call Joni. And Joni doesn't call me.

This is how I know she knows I know.

Dangling Conversations

The next morning, I look for Noah and find Joni instead.

"We've got to talk," she says. I do not argue.

She pulls me into an empty classroom. History's great figures—Eleanor Roosevelt, Mahatma Gandhi, Homer Simpson—look down at us from posters on the walls.

"You saw us. Ted saw us."

It isn't a question, so I don't have to answer.

"What's going on?" I ask instead. Implied in that question is the bigger one: *Why didn't you tell me?*

"I wasn't expecting this to happen."

"Which part? Falling for Chuck, or having to admit it?"

"Don't get hostile."

I sigh. Early signs of defensiveness are not good.

"Look," I say, "you know as well as I do what Chuck did after Infinite Darlene rejected him. He trashed her locker and bad-mouthed her to the whole school."

"He was hurt."

"He was psycho, Joni." (I don't mean to say that; it just comes out. A Friendian Slip.)

Joni shoots me the look I know so well—the same look she shot me when she dyed her hair red in sixth grade and I unsuccessfully tried to pretend it had come out well; the same look she shot me when I tried to convince her (after the first break-up) that getting back together with Ted wasn't the best idea; the same look she shot me when I confessed to her that I was worried I'd never, ever find a boyfriend who loved me the same way I loved him. It's a look that stops all conversation. It's a look that insists, *You're wrong*.

We've been best friends too long to fight each other over this. We both know that.

"So have you talked to Ted?" I ask.

"I wanted to talk to you first."

I think she's doing the wrong thing. My intuition is clear on this: Chuck is bad news. But I know there's nothing I can do to convince her to change her mind. Not without proof.

"So are you, like, Chuck's *girlfriend* now?"

Joni groans. "Remains to be seen, okay? And how are you doing with your Mystery Boy?"

"I have to find him again."

"You lost him?"

"Suppose so."

I say good-bye to Joni and head to Noah's locker. I see Infinite Darlene and duck past her—I'm sure by now she's heard about Joni and Chuck, and I'm sure she'll have loads to say about it.

I also pass Seven and Eight in the halls, their heads leaned gently into each other, their words impossible to overhear. Their real names are Steven and Kate, but no one has called them that for years. They started going out in second grade and haven't been apart since. They are the one-percent of one-percent who meet early on and never need to find anybody else. There's no way to explain it.

Noah is waiting by his locker. No—let me change that. He is *standing* by his locker. There is no sign in his posture or in his gaze that he is waiting for anybody.

"Hey," I say. I scan his features for a reaction. Surprise? Happiness? Anger?

I can't read him.

"Hey," he says back, closing his locker.

"I'm sorry about yesterday," I continue. "Did you get my note?"

He shakes his head. I'm a little thrown.

"Oh. I put a note in your locker. I tried to get here right after school, but ten thousand things got in my way. I really wanted to be here."

He can't read me, either. The confusion is on his face. He doesn't know if I'm being sincere.

"Locker two-six-four, right?"

"Two-six-*three*."

Oops. I apologize on behalf of my pathetic memory and then ask him what he did last night, trying to ease things into a conversation.

"I painted some music. You?"

"Oh, I fought a forest fire." When I don't have anything interesting to say, I usually try to make up something interesting. Then I take one last stab at sounding impressive: "And I started thinking about the Dowager Dance. I'm going to architect it."

"What's the Dowager Dance?" he asks.

I forgot he's new to the school. He has no idea what I'm talking about.

For all he knows, I really do fight forest fires in my free time.

I start giving him answers, explaining away the Dowager Dance and the organizational fury of Lyssa Ling. But instead of giving answers, I want to be asking him questions. What does he mean by "paint some music"? Is he happy I'm here? Does he want me to stop talking? Because I keep talking and talking. I am telling him about the time Lyssa Ling tried to sell bagels with fortunes baked inside them as a sixth-grade fund-raiser, and how the shipment was switched and we got the fortune bagels that were supposed to go to a bachelor party, with XXX-rated slips of paper inserted into the dough. It's a funny story, but somehow I am making it boring. I can't stop in the middle, so I go on and on. Noah doesn't walk away or nod off, but he's certainly not riding my tangent. I'm barely on it myself.

"Thank God I found you!"

It's not Noah saying this. It's Infinite Darlene, right behind me.

"Am I interrupting?" she asks.

Now, I really like Infinite Darlene. But among all my friends, she's usually the last I introduce to new people. I have to prepare them. Because Infinite Darlene doesn't make the best first impression. She seems very full of herself. Which she *is*. It's only after you get to know her better that you realize that somehow she's managed to encompass all her friends within her own self-image, so that when she's acting full of herself, she's actually full of her close friends, too.

There is no way I can expect Noah to understand this.

I try to send Infinite Darlene a look to let her know she's interrupting, without actually telling her out loud.

It doesn't work.

"You must be that boy Paul likes," she says to Noah.

I turn Elmo red.

"And boy," Infinite Darlene continues, "you sure are cute."

The first time Infinite Darlene talked to me like this, I stuttered for days. Noah smiles and takes it in stride.

"Now, are all the girls at this school as nice as you?" he asks. "If so, I'm definitely going to like it here."

He looks right at her as he says it. And I can tell that even Infinite Darlene is a little taken aback, because it's clear he's seeing her just as she wants to be seen. So few people do that.

With two sentences, he's managed to win over my most critical friend.

I am in awe.

I am also mortified by Infinite Darlene's declaration of my

liking. Sure, I'm about as smooth as a camel's back … but I was still trying to win him over with my own sweet plan (whatever that might be).

Of course, Infinite Darlene will only let a beat last so long before stepping in again.

"Is this awful, vile rumor I hear actually true? Break it to me gently."

"Do you mind if I derail for a second?" I ask Noah, then quickly add, "Please stay."

"No problem," he says.

That settled, I face Infinite Darlene. In heels, she is easily six inches taller than me. In an effort to break it to her gently, I talk to her chin.

"It appears that Joni has started something with—"

"Stop!" Infinite Darlene interrupts, stepping back and holding up her hand. "I can't take any more. Why, Paul? *Why?*"

"I don't know."

"He's scum."

I am not about to argue with a football captain who has long fingernails.

"Haven't I taught her *anything*?" Infinite Darlene is clearly exasperated. "I mean, I *know* she has bad taste. But this is like licking the bottom of your stiletto."

Clearly, Infinite Darlene still feels some hostility toward Chuck.

"I have to find that girl and talk some sense into her," she concludes. I put up a show of trying to dissuade her, but we both know there's no way I'm going to stop her. She leaves in a huff.

"Friend of yours?" Noah asks, eyebrow raised.

I nod.

"I'll bet she's always like that."

I nod again.

"I feel very calm in comparison."

"We all do," I assure him. "This is the kind of stuff I was dealing with yesterday when I should've been here."

"Does this happen often?"

"Not this specific thing, but there's usually something like it."

"Do you think you could escape the crisis for a few hours this afternoon?"

Since Infinite Darlene blew my cover so thoroughly, I decide to take a risk.

"You're not asking me just because I like you?"

He smiles. "The thought never crossed my mind."

We don't say any more than that. I mean, we say things—we make plans and all. But the subject of us is dropped back into signals and longing.

We make plans for after school.

I'm going to help him paint some music.

Painting Music

Noah's house is in a different part of town than mine, but the neighborhood looks just the same. Each house has a huge welcome mat of lawn sitting in front of it, bordered by a driveway on one side and a hedge on the other. It should be boringly predictable, but it's not really. The houses are personalized— a blush of geraniums around the front stoop, a pair of shutters painted to echo the blue sky. In Noah's yard, the hedges have been made into the shape of lightbulbs—the legacy of the former owner, Noah tells me.

He lives close to the high school, so we walk the bendily cross-hatched roads together. He asks me how long I've lived in town, and I tell him I've lived here my whole life.

"What's that like?" he asks.

"I don't really have anything to compare it to," I say after a moment's thought. "This is all I know."

Noah explains that his family has moved four times in the last ten years. This is meant to be the final stop—now his parents travel everywhere for business instead of making the family move to the nearest headquarter city.

"I'm so dislocated," Noah confesses.

"You're here now," I tell him.

If my family were to move (honestly, I can't imagine it, but I'm stating it here for the sake of argument), I think it would take us about three years to unpack all of our boxes. Noah's family, however, has put everything in its place. We walk through the front door and I'm amazed at how immaculate everything is. The furniture has settled into its new home; the only thing the house lacks is clutter. We walk into the living room—and it's one of those living rooms that look like nobody ever lives in them.

We head to the kitchen for a snack. Noah's sister is sitting alert at the corner table, like a parent waiting up late at night for a kid to come home.

"You're late," she says. "You missed Mom's call."

She must be in eighth grade—maybe seventh. She's old enough to wear make-up, but she hasn't figured out yet how to wear it well.

"Is she going to call back?" Noah asks.

"Maybe." End of conversation.

Noah reaches out for the mail on the table, sifting through the catalogs and bulk mail for something worthwhile.

"Paul, this is my sister, Claudia," he says as he separates the recyclable from the nonrecyclable. "Claudia, this is Paul."

"Nice to meet you," I say.

"Nice to meet you, too. Don't hurt him like Pitt did, okay?"

Noah's annoyed now. "Claudia, go to your room," he says, giving up on the mail.

"You're not the boss of me."

"I can't believe you just said that. What are you, six years old?"

"Excuse me, but aren't you the one who just said 'Go to your room'? And by the way, Pitt wrecked you. Or have you forgotten?"

It's clear Noah hasn't forgotten. And neither, to her credit, has Claudia.

Satisfied by this turn of conversation, Claudia drops the subject.

"I just made a smoothie pitcher," she tells us as she gets up from the table. "You can have some, but leave at least half."

Once she's out of the room, Noah asks me if I have a little sister. I tell him I have an older brother, which isn't really the same thing.

"Different methods of beating you up," Noah says.

I nod.

After drinking some of Claudia's mango-cherry-vanilla concoction, Noah leads me up the back stairs to his room.

Before we reach his door, he says, "I hope you don't mind whimsy."

In truth, I'd never given whimsy much thought before.

Then I see his room and I know exactly what he means.

I don't know where to begin, both in looking at it and describing it. The ceiling is a swirl of just about any color you'd care to imagine. But it doesn't seem like it was painted with different colors—it looks like it appeared at once, as a whole. One wall is covered with Matchbox cars glued in different directions, with a town and roads drawn in the background. His music collection hangs on a swing from the ceiling; his stereo is elevated on a pedestal of postcards from absurd places—Botswana, the Kansas City International Airport, an Elvis convention. His books are kept on freestanding shelves hung at different angles on a sea-green wall. They defy gravity, as good books should. His bed is in the middle of the room, but can be rolled effortlessly into any corner. His windowshades are made from old bubblegum wrappers, arranged into a design.

"You did all this in two months?" I ask. It has taken me fifteen years to decorate my room, and it isn't nearly as intricate or . . . whimsical. I'd like it to be.

Noah nods. "Since I don't know many people here, I guess I had time."

He goes to the stereo and hits a few buttons. He smiles a little nervously.

"This is very cool," I assure him. "It's a very cool room. Mine isn't nearly as cool."

"I doubt that," he says.

It's not that the weirdness of the moment doesn't strike me. I realize that the two of us don't really know each other. And at the same time, there's that comforting, unattributable vibe we're both feeling, which intuitively tells us that we *should* get to know each other. By showing me his room, he's giving me a glimpse of his soul. I am nervous about giving in return.

In the middle of the book-angled wall is a very narrow door—it can't be more than two feet wide. "This way," Noah says, guiding me toward it. He opens it up, revealing a guard of shirts. Then he disappears inside.

I follow. The door closes behind me. There is no light.

We push through the closet, which is unusually deep. Because it's so narrow, Noah's clothes are hung in layers. I push through the hangered row of his shirts and find myself folded between two dangling sweaters.

"Are we going to Narnia?" I ask.

I squeeze to a crawl to follow him through a vent-like passage. Then his legs stretch up—he's standing in a new passage, pulling himself up a rope ladder, up toward a trap door. By my reckoning, we're headed into a corner of the attic. But I can't be sure.

As the trap door is raised, light streams down on us. I am surrounded by brick. I am in the middle of an old chimney.

At the top of the rope ladder is a white room. There is one window, one cabinet, and two speakers. An easel stands in the middle of the room, with a blank square of waiting paper.

"This is where I paint," Noah says as he sets up a second easel. "Nobody else is allowed up here. My parents promised me that when we moved. You're really the first person to see it."

The floor is paint-splattered—trails of color, spots of shape.

Even the white walls have hints of vermilion, azure, and gold. Noah doesn't seem to mind.

I am a little worried, since the last time I painted there were numbers on the paper telling me which colors to use. I am an ace doodler, but other than that my artistic repertoire is quite limited.

"Jesus died for our sins," Noah says solemnly.

"What?!?" I reply, choking back my thoughts.

"I was just seeing if you were listening. Your face went far away for a second."

"Well, I'm back now."

"Good." He hands me a vase of brushes and an ice-cube tray of paints. "Now we can start."

"Wait!" I protest. "I don't know what to do."

He smiles. "Just listen to the music and paint. Follow the sound. Don't think about rules. Don't worry about getting it perfect. Just let the song carry you."

"But what about instructions?"

"There are no other instructions."

He walks over to the speakers and plugs them into the wall. The music begins, drifting into the room like a perfumed scent. A piano tinkles in jazz cadences. A trumpet chimes in. And then the voice—this wonderful voice—begins to croon.

"There's a somebody I'm longing to see. . . ."

"Who is this?" I ask.

"Chet Baker."

He's marvelous.

"Don't get lost in the words," Noah says, ready to paint. "Follow the sounds."

At first I don't know what this means. I dip my brush into a velvety purple. I raise it to the canvas and listen to the music. Chet Baker's voice is sinuous, floaty. I touch the brush to the paper and try to make it soar in time with the song. I swoop it down, then up again. I am not painting a shape. I am painting the tune.

The song continues. I wash my brush and try different colors. The sunflower yellow settles in patches, while the tomato red flirts over the lines of purple. Another song begins. I reach for a blue the color of oceans.

"... I'm so lucky to be the one you run to see...."

I close my eyes and add the blue to my painting. When I open my eyes, I look over to Noah and see he's been glancing at me. I think he knows I understand.

Another song. I am now able to see things in my painting—the hint of a wing, the undertow of a tide.

Noah surprises me by speaking.

"Have you always known?" he asks. I know immediately what he's talking about.

"Pretty much so, yeah," I answer. "You?"

He nods, eyes still on the canvas, his brush a mark of blue.

"Has it been easy for you?"

"Yes," I tell him, because it's the truth.

"It hasn't always been easy for me," he says, then says no more.

I stop painting and watch him for a moment. He is concentrating on the music now, moving his brush in an arc. He is completely in tune with the trumpet that solos above the beat. His mood reflects indigo. Is it heartbreak that makes him sad (I remember his sister's comment in the kitchen), or is it something else?

He senses my stillness and turns to me. There is something in his expression the moment before he speaks—I cannot tell whether it's vulnerability or doubt. Is he unsure about himself or unsure about me?

"Let me see what you've done," he says.

I shake my head. "Not 'til the song is over."

But when the song is over, I'm still not satisfied.

"It doesn't look right," I tell him as the next song begins.

"Let's see," he says. Part of me wants to block his view, blot out what I've created. But I let him see anyway.

He stands next to me, looking at the music I've painted. When he speaks, Chet Baker's horn highlights his words.

"This is splendid," he says.

He is so close to me. All I can feel is his presence. It is in the air surrounding us, the music surrounding us, and all my thoughts.

I am still holding the paintbrush. He reaches for my hand and lifts it gently.

"Here," he whispers, guiding me across the paper, leaving an auburn trail.

"It's only twilight, I watch 'til the star breaks through. . . ."

The brush covers its distance. We both know when it ends. Our hands lower together, still holding on.

We do not let go.

We stand there looking. His hand over mine. Our breathing.

We leave everything unsaid.

The song ends. Another begins. This one is a blast of upbeat.

"Let's get lost. . . ."

Our hands separate. I turn to him. He smiles and walks back to his easel, taking up his brush. I follow him to peek over his shoulder.

I am floored.

His painting is not an abstraction. He has only used one color, a near-black green. The woman in the painting is dancing with her eyes closed. She is all that he's drawn, but all you need is her figure to know what is going on. She is on a dance floor, and she is dancing alone.

"Wow," I murmur.

He bashfully turns away. "Let's finish," he says.

So I head back to my own easel, stepping on the marks of paint I have already left on the floor. We lose ourselves to the songs once more. At one point, he briefly sings along. I do not stop to listen, but instead work it into my canvas. My flights of color are meeting his dancer somewhere in the middle of the room. We do not need to speak to be aware of each other's presence.

We stay this way until twilight colors the window and the hour calls me home.

Chuck Waggin'

"So did you kiss him?" Joni asks first thing. It never takes her very long to get to the point. She's going to ask all the questions about Noah that I'm not going to ask about Chuck.

Now, I am not one to kiss and tell, but Joni's heard about every single boy I've ever kissed. Sometimes I've told her two minutes after the fact; other times it's come up years later, as my way of proving she doesn't know *everything* about me. From my first spin-the-bottle kiss with Cody to the final, conflicted kiss-off kiss with Kyle, Joni's been the one I've shared the stories with. So it comes as no surprise to have her question me now, on the phone, fifteen minutes after I've come home from Noah's.

"That's none of your business," I say.

"Is that a 'none of your business' yes, or a 'none of your business' no?"

"I don't want to tell you."

"So it's 'no.'"

I don't know how to explain it to her. It's not that I didn't want to kiss Noah. And I think he wanted to kiss me. But we left the moment to silence instead. The promise of a kiss will carry us forward.

Since I don't say anything more, Joni lets the subject drop. Much to my surprise, she picks up the subject of Kyle instead.

"Has Kyle spoken to you?" she asks, in a way that makes it clear that Kyle has spoken to *her*.

"Does saying hi in the halls count?"

"Well, it's a step."

Joni always liked Kyle. She liked his confusion, his woundedness, his bafflement . . . the same things I liked about him, as well as his natural charm and his sincerity. When these things turned against me, I think Joni was almost as hurt as I was. She'd trusted him with me. He let both of us down.

The thing is, Joni got over it easier than I did. I guess hurt is essentially a firsthand emotion. When Kyle started talking the straight-and-narrow, she was willing to believe him. Sure, he'd started dating girls—but those relationships rarely lasted longer than a PSAT prep course. After they broke up, they never stayed friends.

"I think he wants to talk to you. I *know* he wants to talk to you."

"What could he possibly want to talk about?"

"I think he feels bad," Joni tells me.

I wonder what *feeling bad* means in this particular situation. I can't imagine it's the same *feeling bad* as when you lend your boyfriend your favorite ultra-comfortable sweater and then find him wearing it as he says that the only feeling he can muster toward you is annoyance, and then wearing it again a week later as he walks past you in the halls, pretending you don't exist as he flirts with the one girl who had been after him the whole time you'd been going out. It can't be the same *feeling bad* as knowing that the sweater—the sweater you looked best in, the sweater you felt best in, the sweater you now fear he'll be wearing when you see him in between classes—is sitting at the bottom of a closet, where he doesn't give a damn about it, or has been given away to some other person he's pretended to love.

Perhaps I need to polish my vindictive streak, but I don't want him to feel that bad. Because I've seen him—I've seen the loneliness behind his eyes, the way he'll stop in the halls unsure of where to make the next step.

Since he made me feel invisible, I spent months wishing he'd disappear. Now it feels like I've gotten half my wish. His spirit has gone. His body remains.

"How's he doing?" I ask Joni, despite my better instincts.

"I don't know if he's happy. But he's got a cat."

"A cat?" As far as I know, Kyle hates animals.

"He took in a stray."

"How ironic," I say, even though I know Kyle is one of the few people in our school who doesn't do irony on a breathing basis.

"Chuck has a cat, too," Joni volunteers.

Which is, of course, her way of saying she wants to talk about Chuck.

I brace myself.

"He's really not that bad," she says.

"Who? Kyle?" I'm not going to make this easy. That's my right as her best friend.

"No, Chuck. I really like him."

"I'm sure if I spent more time with him, I'd get to know him better," I say, choosing my words very carefully.

"And I'm sure I'll like Noah," Joni replies.

I freeze for a moment, afraid she'll propose a double date. Instead she says that she, Chuck, and I should head out to lunch together tomorrow.

Because she's my best friend, I say yes.

Only seniors are allowed to leave campus for lunch, but that doesn't stop the rest of us from going out anyway. Our principal's wife owns the sub shop down the street, and I think she'd be out of business in a second without the support of cafeteria-fleeing sophomores and juniors. The seniors can manage to drive somewhere better, but the underclassmen basically have two walking-distance choices.

Whenever I go out, I skip the sub shop and head to the Veggie D's on the other side of the street. The Veggie D's used to be your usual processed-slaughterhouse fast-food joint, but a few years ago a bunch of vegetarians launched a boycott and soon the chain lost its link. A local food co-op took over the building, keeping all the fixtures intact. They even made the workers keep the uniforms, only with a leaf pinned where the corporate logo used to be.

Since Joni can drive, we could conceivably go somewhere else. But I want to be within departure range this time, just in case Chuck makes me want to go away.

What I really want to do is, of course, spend as much time as I can with Noah. This is sudden and unusual for me, but I decide to ride it. I want to know more. I tell him this when I see him at his locker before first period. He tells me not to worry about lunch—we have a whole weekend coming up, and all the time it offers. Without saying a word, we arrange to pass notes between each class. Between first and second, we meet at my locker. Between second and third, we head to his. And so on. Reading about his boredom in math class, or the dream he had last night about penguins, or his mom's phone call from some indistinguishable airport lounge, I begin to learn about him in the first person. I try to write back in the same way, giving a little clue to myself in every sentence. For him, I recall my grandmother's smile, the time Jay and I dressed as each other for Halloween (none of the neighbors got it), Mrs. Benchly's words on my kindergarten evaluation. It's all very random, but that's what my thoughts are like. I can tell from Noah's notes that we have a compatible randomness.

I've told Joni to meet me (with Chuck) in front of my locker. In retrospect, this is a stupid, stupid decision. Because as soon as they show up, Infinite Darlene walks past, clicking her tongue and swishing away. Then, even worse, as Chuck and I are nodding hey, Ted appears behind him. He stops for a second and takes a good look at what we're doing. He, too, walks away irate, betrayed. I feel like a dust mite. And I still have to get through lunch.

Chuck is a short guy but he works out a lot, so as a result he's built like a fire hydrant. Most of the time he acts like a fire hydrant, too. Conversation is not his strong suit. In fact, I'm not sure it's a suit he owns.

So it's Joni and I who chat the whole way to Veggie D's. I doubt Chuck is very happy about our destination—he strikes me as a carnivore—but he doesn't really protest. I find myself liking him okay when his mouth is shut.

After Joni orders a VegHummus and a six-piece Tofu Veg-Nuggets, Chuck and I both opt for the Double Lentil Tempeh Burger with a side order of fries. I get a smoothie, but Chuck goes for a VegCola.

"I don't like fruit," he explains. "No offense."

Only his "no offense" offends me.

But because he's my best friend's new boyfriend, I let it slide.

(For now.)

Eating makes Chuck talk more. He and Joni are sitting across from me, holding hands while they chew. They are exactly the same height.

Since Chuck's a sporting guy, I think it's only fair that I keep score of his conversation.

"So I hear you're planning that dance?" he says. (Five points: He's showing an interest in me instead of prattling on about himself.)

"Well," I reply, "Lyssa Ling's planning it. I'm merely the architect."

"Whatever." (Minus two points.) "If you want to sneak in a keg, my dad knows a supplier and I can probably get you one cheap." (Plus three points for helpfulness, minus two for inappropriateness.)

"Chuck's dad has the biggest liquor collection I've ever seen," Joni chimes in.

"But he doesn't drink any," Chuck continues. "He just likes the bottles." (Plus three for an interesting father.) "How lame is that?" (Minus four for not realizing it.)

"How's football going this year?" I ask.

Chuck's eyes light up. (Joni would be lucky if the mention of her name ever got such a response.) "I think we really have a chance to take State. Watchung is weak, and South Orange's best player graduated last year. Livingston's best player is on the verge of indictment, and Hanover hasn't fielded a decent team since their coach was a player. Caldwell's the one to watch, but I feel like we could take them if we keep our guard up. Our practices have been *so rockin'* lately. We're tight, you know. Real tight." (Ten points for passion. So what if it's football he's talking about—if you can be so engaged and excited by the thing you do, you get points.)

"The only problem," Chuck continues, "is our goddamn quarterback. He's totally psycho."

Minus twenty points. Chuck knows I'm friends with Infinite Darlene. So why is he slamming her? Doesn't he know any better?

He goes on. "He's more worried about breaking his nails than throwing the pigskin." (At the sound of the word *pigskin,* half the Veggie D's customers turn around and give us a nasty look.) "He should just enter the beauty contests instead of heading onto the gridiron, if you know what I mean."

Oh, I know what he means. He means: *I had a crush on the quarterback and she didn't have a crush back, so now I'm going to bad-mouth her since I can't undo the crush I once had.* I can see right through every word he's said, because I've witnessed Infinite Darlene on the football field. When she is on the hundred yards, she is all business. She will break her nails and blotch her mascara and sweat and grunt and shove and do whatever it takes to get to the end zone. She is all precision, no distraction. It's probably what attracted Chuck in the first place.

I stop keeping score, because in my book, Chuck's already lost the game. I look over to Joni for confirmation . . . but she just smiles at me. As if to say, *Isn't he cute?*

Chuck asks me about movies, because Joni must have told him I like movies. But he only asks me about the movies he's seen, so he can give his own opinion. Opinions like "That helicopter chase was intense" and "She can't act, but she sure is a babe." I look over at Joni again.

She's nodding along.

She's not saying much.

She holds his hand and looks happy.

Part of me wants to scream and part of me wants to laugh, both for the same reason: This is an impossible situation. Joni doesn't need my approval, but she wants it, in the same way that I would want hers. But if I approve, I'm lying. And if I don't, I'll be shutting myself out of a major part of her life.

"I really liked that article you wrote for the paper about the hate crimes law," Chuck is now saying. Does he realize he's lost me? Is he trying to win me back? That effort alone would count for something, if not a lot.

I usually think our thirty-four-minute lunch period is too short. Now I feel it's just right. We sort and throw out our garbage, then head back to school. Since it's Friday, we talk about our weekend plans. For some reason, I decide not to mention Noah. In contrast, every plan Joni and Chuck mention starts with the word *we*. Usually Joni and I would plan a point to connect over the weekend. This time, neither of us makes that move.

I notice this. I wonder if she does, too.

In between sixth and seventh periods, before I get a note from Noah, Ted comes right up to me and calls me a traitor. Now, I've never felt any allegiance to Ted before. In fact, I was usually a big fan when Joni decided to dump him. But today it feels different. Today I *do* feel like a traitor, although maybe the old Joni is the one I've betrayed.

"You're taking sides," Ted spits out at me.

"I'm not," I try to convince him. "And I thought you said you didn't care."

"I don't. But I didn't think you'd be supporting her stupid decision, Gay Boy. I thought you had some sense."

I can't tell him I agree, because then word will get back to Joni and she'll know how I really feel. So I stand there and take his wave of anger. I make it clear I don't know what to do.

He stares me down for a second, says "Fine," then heads off to his next class.

I wonder if it's possible to start a new relationship without hurting someone else. I wonder if it's possible to have happiness without it being at someone else's expense.

Then I see Noah coming over to me with a note folded in the shape of a crane.

And I think, yes, it's possible.

I think I can fall for him without hurting anybody.

A Walk in the Park

Our plan for Saturday is to not have a plan for Saturday. This un-eases me a little, since I'm a pretty big fan of plans. But for Noah, I'm willing to try a planless day out.

He's going to come by my house at noon. I'm totally fine with this—until I realize it means he'll be meeting my family.

Now, don't get me wrong—I like my family. While many of my friends' parents have been arguing, divorcing, and custody-sharing, my parents have been planning family vacations and setting the table for family dinners. They're usually pretty good about meeting my boyfriends, although I think they're always a little confused about who's my boyfriend and who is just a friend who happens to be a boy. (It took them a couple months to catch on that Tony and I weren't a thing.)

No, my fear isn't that my parents are going to push Noah out the door with a cattle prod. Instead, I'm afraid they'll be too friendly and give too much of me away before I can reveal it. As a precaution, I lock all the family photo albums in a drawer and decide to tell them Noah is "a new friend" without specifying anything else. Jay, who (like any older brother) loves to see me squirm, is the big wild card—he's off at tennis practice, but there's no telling when he'll come home.

I clean my room thoroughly, then mess it up a little so it won't look so clean. I worry that it's not whimsical enough. Instead, it's the museum of my whole life, from my Snoopys with their wardrobes to the mirror ball my parents got me when I graduated from fifth grade to the Wilde books still open-winged on my floor from last week's English report.

This is my life, I think. I am an accumulation of objects.

The doorbell rings precisely at noon, as if it were attached to a grandfather clock.

Noah is right on time. And he's brought me flowers.

I want to cry. I am such a sap, but right now I am so happy. Hyacinth and jacaranda and a dozen other flowers that I cannot begin to name. An alphabet of flowers. He is giving them to me, smiling and saying hi, reaching out and putting them in my hand. His shirt shimmers a little in the sunlight. His hair is as unkempt as ever. He teeters a little on the front step, waiting to be invited in.

I lean forward and kiss him. The flowers crush between our shirts. I touch his lips, I breathe him in. I close my eyes, I open them. He is surprised, I can tell. I am surprised, too. He kisses me back with a kiss like a smile.

It's very nice.

Actually, it's wonderful.

"Hello," I say.

"Hello," Noah says back.

I hear footsteps coming down from upstairs. My parents.

"Come in," I say. I hold the flowers in one hand and swing my other hand behind me. Noah takes it as he walks through the door.

"Hello there," my parents say together as they reach the bottom of the stairs. In one glance they see the flowers, and me and Noah holding hands. They can immediately figure out that Noah is more than just a new friend.

I don't care.

My mother instinctively looks at Noah's teeth as he says, "It's a pleasure to meet you." I can't really blame her: she's a dentist, and she can't help doing it. The biggest fight we ever had was when I refused to get braces. I wouldn't even open my mouth to let the orthodontist see my teeth. He threatened to put the braces on my closed mouth, and as far as I was concerned, that was that. I won't be bullied into anything, and I have the crooked teeth to prove it. My mother is constantly mortified by this, although she's nice enough not to mention it anymore.

Because I am my mother's son, I noticed right away that Noah's bottom front teeth overlap a little. Because I am not *entirely* my mother's son, I find this flaw to be beautiful.

"It's a pleasure to meet you," my father tells Noah, putting his hand out to shake. Noah and I disengage so he can make a good impression. My father has, I believe, the perfect handshake, neither fish nor fist. The handshake is his great equalizer—by the time he pulls his hand back, you feel you're right on his level. He's honed this craft in his years as the director of philanthropy at Puffy Soft, a national toiletries chain. His job is to take a portion of the profits that come from selling TP and give the money away to underfunded school programs. He is a walking example of why our country is such a strange and unbelievable place.

Noah is checking out our living room, and I am getting a look through his eyes. I realize how strange the wallpaper print is, and how all the pillows from the couch are in a pile on the floor, betraying the fact that someone (probably my father) just had a lie-down.

"Do you guys want pancakes?" my mother asks.

"My family believes breakfast can be served at any meal," I explain to Noah.

"I'm all for it," he says. "I mean, if you want to."

"Do you?" I ask.

"If you do."

"Are you sure?"

"Are you?"

"I'll make the pancakes," my mother interjects. "You guys have about ten minutes to decide if you want to eat them."

She heads into the kitchen. My father points to the flowers.

"You should put those in water," he says. "They're lovely."

Noah blushes. I blush. But I don't move. I'm not sure if Noah is ready to be alone with my father yet. Still, if I say that, I'll offend both of them. So I head for the nearest vase.

It's not until I'm alone—it's not until I'm given a sensory pause—that the full enormity of what's happened hits me. Two minutes ago, I was kissing Noah and he was kissing me back. Now he's in the living room with my father. The boy I just kissed is talking to my father. The boy I want to kiss again is waiting for my mother to serve pancakes.

I must fight the urge to freak.

I find an old *Dallas* thermos and put the flowers inside. Their color complements Charlene Tilton's eyes nicely. The thermos is a relic from the early years of my parents' everlasting courtship.

Now that the flowers are in place, I'm feeling a little better. Then I hear my father's voice from the other room.

"Look at how big his thighs are here!"

Oh, no. The photo shrine. How could I have forgotten?

Sure enough, I walk in and find Noah framed by frames, the story of my transformation from pudgy to gawky to awkward to lanky to awkward again, all in the space of fifteen years.

Luckily, the thighs in question are on my six-month-old self.

"Pancakes are almost ready!" my mother calls.

We head to the kitchen. My father takes the lead, so I get to hang back a moment with Noah. He looks perfectly amused.

"Do you mind?" I ask.

"I'm having fun," he assures me.

I know that other people's families are always more amusing than your own. But I'm not used to my family being the other person's family.

"States or countries?" my father asks as we reach the kitchen.

"You tell me," my mother replies.

I have no idea why I'm surprised by this. It must be Noah's presence that makes me expect normal from my parents, even when I know this is rarely the case. Whenever my mom makes pancakes, they are usually the shape of states or countries. It's how I learned geography. If this seems a little bizarre, let me emphasize here—I am not talking about blobs of batter that look like California when you squint. No, I'm talking coastlines and mountain ranges and little star imprints where the capital should be. Because my mom drills teeth for a living, she is very, very precise. She can draw a straight line without a ruler and fold a napkin in perfect symmetry. In this regard, I am nothing at all like her. Most of the time, I feel like a perpetual smudge. My lines all curve. I tend to connect the wrong dots.

(Joni tells me this isn't true, that I say I'm a smudge because I can see my mother's precision growing inside of me. But let me tell you—I could never make two separate pancakes that fit together the way my mother's Texas and Oklahoma do.)

My parents steal glimpses of Noah. He steals glimpses of them. I watch them all openly, and nobody seems to mind.

"How long have you been living in town?" my father asks, perfectly conversational.

Just then, my brother busts into the room, leaving a trail of tennis sweat.

"Who are you?" Jay asks, pouring a little syrup on Minnesota before lifting the whole thing into his mouth.

"Noah." I like that he doesn't explain any further, and that he resists saying "It's nice to meet you" until he figures out whether such a statement is true.

"Another gay boy?" my brother says to me, then sighs. "Man, why can't you ever bring home a really cute sophomore girl to fall desperately in love with me? Do you *have* any cute girlfriends? Dogface doesn't count." (He and Joni go way back; she calls him Dungbrain.)

Before I can say anything, Noah steps in. "I was going to set you up with my sister," he says, "but you just blew your chance."

Jay stops chewing and pauses before making a grab for Arkansas. "Is she hot?" he asks. "Your sister?"

"She's malaria hot," Noah tells him. "Isn't that right, Paul?"

"I had to look twice when I saw her," I chime in. "And I don't even like girls that way."

Jay nods in approval. My mother swats his hand with a spatula as he goes to stick his finger in the leftover batter. My father looks at us both, wondering how he can have two sons who make him feel so midway.

Finally, Jay starts to talk about practice, and Noah and I get our share of the edible nation. My mom asks us if we want more ("I can do provinces, if you'd like"), but we both take a pass.

We're ready to leave the house.

"I'd like to meet her!" my brother shouts out as we head for the door (after thanking my mom profusely). It takes me a second to realize he's talking about Noah's sister.

We have a laugh about that as we bound down my front path.

"Where now?" we ask each other at the same time.

Both of us hesitate, not wanting to be the first to answer.

Finally, we can't take it.

"The park," we say at the same time.

Which is very cool.

We hold hands as we walk through town. If anybody notices, nobody cares. I know we all like to think of the heart as the center of the body, but at this moment, every conscious part of me is in the

65

hand that he holds. It is through that hand, that feeling, that I experience everything else. The only things I notice around me are the good things—the mesmerizing tunes spilling out from the open door of the record store; the older man and the even older woman sitting on a park bench, sharing a blintz; the seven-year-old leaping from sidewalk square to sidewalk square, teetering and shifting to avoid stepping on a crack.

As if by agreement, although we haven't made a plan, we head for the paddleboat pavilion. A lone duck greets our arrival. To our right, the skatepunks swoosh-ride on a ramp made of hemp, speeding to queercore thrash and the sound of their own bodies merging with the wind. To our left, a posse of Joy Scouts takes guitar lessons from a retired monk. (We used to have a troop of Boy Scouts, but when the Boy Scouts decided gays had no place in their ranks, our Scouts decided the organization had no place in our town; they changed their name and continued on.)

The pond's surface is like a wrinkled blue shirt, with small buoy-buttons marking the distance of water. The paddleboat wrangler has named the boats after his seven daughters. From the time I was little, I've always chosen Trixie, because she's orange and has the funniest name. This time the paddleboat wrangler lifts his eyebrow at me because I go along when Noah chooses the light green Adaline. I like the idea of following his whims. I like the idea of going with him into a boat I've never been in before. Trixie has seen me with Joni and Kyle, other friends and other guys; she has also seen me paddle alone for hours, trying to sort out my problems by leaving a wake. Adaline doesn't know any of my secrets.

Noah and I start to talk about our favorite books and our favorite paintings—sharing our Indicators, hoping the other person will appreciate them as much. I know this is a normal early-date thing to do, but it's still unusual to me; since I've lived in the same town my whole life, I'm used to dating people I already know well.

There are always smaller mysteries to unravel, but I often have the general picture right in my mind when the dating begins. Noah, however, is entirely new to me. And I am entirely new to him. It would be so easy to lie — to make my favorites the same as his, or to pick more impressive choices. And yet I tell the truth. I want this all to be the truth.

The paddling pond isn't very large. We intersect it at constantly different angles. We shift direction like we shift conversation — in slow, subtle, natural ways.

"I don't do this very often," Noah says to me. "You know, go out."

"Neither do I," I assure him. It's mostly true, although not quite as true as what he's said to me.

"It's been a while."

"What happened?" I ask, because I sense he wants me to ask.

But maybe I've sensed wrong. He stops paddling for a second and his looks dark-cloud on me.

"You don't have to tell me," I say quietly.

He shakes his head. "No . . . it's okay. It's one of those things that you don't want to come up, but you know it has to come up, and then when it does you hope that once you've talked about it, it won't be that important anymore. It's really not a very interesting story. I liked this guy a lot. And I thought he liked me a lot, but in truth he didn't really like me at all. He was my first boyfriend, and I made him my everything — he was my new life, my new love, my new compass point. I guess that's the danger with firsts — you lose all sense of proportion. So I made a fool of myself, even though I didn't realize it at the time. I was so _devoted_ to him." His "devoted" is italicized by sarcasm, underlined by hurt. "And he didn't really care. He was a year older than me, and for a while I used that as an excuse for not knowing he was cheating on me with roughly half his grade. I thought I could see him so well. But I didn't see him at all, really. And he didn't even try to see me.

"Finally, he told me. And the really screwed-up thing is, when he told me, it was one of the most caring things he'd ever done for me—at least in a while. I guess he got a ninth-inning conscience. He told me I was great, and that because I was great there were some things I needed to know. And of course I wondered for months afterwards why, if I was so great, he had to go play on me. I felt so destroyed. More than I should have—but I only realize that now. It was so unfair. It was so *unkind*.

"I was still getting over it when my parents decided to move. In a lot of ways, I was relieved. I couldn't stand seeing him in the halls. He was this constant, living reminder of my biggest mistake."

I nod, and sift through my noticings. I notice that Noah hasn't mentioned this boy by name (even though I'm sure it's Pitt, the one Noah's sister mentioned before). I notice that Noah has been facing me the whole time instead of looking to the water or in the direction we're paddling; he is not just telling this story—he is giving it to me. I notice the hope and expectation in his eyes, the desire to have me understand exactly what he's saying. Which I do, to some extent. It reminds me of my time with Kyle, without really being the story of me and Kyle. Kyle was certainly unfair, and he was certainly unkind, but his intentions were more confused, less deliberate. Or so I like to think.

I tell Noah a little about Kyle—how could I not?—and about some of the other disastrous dates I've had. More the funny stories than the pained ones. The blind date with the boy in seventh grade who tucked his shirt into his underwear and his pants into his socks, just to be "more secure." The boy at sleep-away camp who giggled whenever I used an adverb. The Finnish exchange student who wanted me to pretend to be Molly Ringwald whenever we went out.

There is an unspoken recognition as we share these stories—we can talk about the bad dates and bad boyfriends because this is not a bad date, and we will not be bad boyfriends. We forget the fact that many of our earlier relationships (definitely with Kyle, probably with Pitt) started in the same way. We pencil-sketch our previous life so we can contrast it to the Technicolor of the moment.

This is how we proclaim a beginning.

We talk about school and we talk about the other kids in town. I talk about my brother and he talks about his sister. After a while, our legs are getting tired and we're running out of new angles to cross the pond. So we stop paddling and let ourselves drift. We push our legs forward and slump in the seats. I put my arm around his shoulders and he puts his arm around mine. We close our eyes and feel the sun glow on our faces. I open my eyes first and study the curve of his jaw, the smoothness of his cheeks, the random arrangement of his hair. I imprint him with my shadow as I lean in closer. I kiss him once, but it lasts a long time.

This, too, is how we proclaim a beginning.

The sun starts to dip lower, and we return to clock time. We make our way to the paddleboat pavilion, where the paddleboat wrangler gives us an approving nod for bringing Adaline safely home.

As we cross back through the park we see more people, mostly regulars. The Old Queen sits at his bench, reminiscing about Broadway in the 1920s. Two benches away, the Young Punk shouts loudly about Sid and Nancy and the birth of revolt. They rarely find themselves without a willing audience, but when the foot traffic slows, the Old Queen and the Young Punk sit together and share memories of events that happened long before they were born.

I explain this all to Noah, and I love the wonder that shows in his eyes. We continue to tour through the town, and everything is new to him: the I Scream Parlor, which shows horror movies as you wait for your double dip; the elementary school playground, where I used to tell the jungle gym all my secrets; the Pink Floyd shrine in our local barber's backyard. I know people always talk about living in the middle of nowhere—there's always another place (some city, some foreign country) they'd rather be. But it's moments like this that I feel like I live in the middle of somewhere. My somewhere.

We walk rings around Noah's neighborhood, and then when we enter it, we walk rings around his block. He has to be home at a certain time, and it's unclear to me whether I'm being invited along.

"Both my parents will be there," he says, to explain his hesitation.

"I can handle them," I reply.

He's still unsure.

"They're not like your parents," he warns.

"That's a good thing!"

"I don't think so."

Suddenly I'm picturing Tony's parents, who need to think that Joni and I are safely dating in order for Tony to leave the house with us. They think that Tony's personality is simply a matter of switches, and that if they find the right one, they can turn off his attraction to other guys and put him back on the road to God.

"Do they know you're gay?" I ask Noah.

"They couldn't care less. But with other things—well, their priorities are a little weird."

We've stopped circling now—we're in front of his house.

"What the heck," he says. We walk inside and he calls out, "I'm home!"

"Who cares?" Claudia yells back from a distant room.

We head to the kitchen for ice pops. I can't help but notice three credit cards sitting on the counter.

"Mom!? Dad?! I'm home!"

Claudia trundles into the room. "You are, but they're not. They say hi, though. We can order whatever we want. Just use the United card, because they need the mileage there more than on Continental."

"Where'd they go?" Noah asks.

"Out to dinner, to celebrate. Mom finally got admitted to the Commander Club. She can now use the Commander Club lounges at all major airports, *including* free coffee and Internet access."

As Noah ponders this, Claudia pulls the ice pop out of his hand and takes it for herself. She walks back into her distant room; I can hear her footsteps fade, and then the TV blare up.

"I guess we have to stay in," Noah says.

"Isn't she old enough to be alone by herself?" I ask.

"I'm not worried about her being alone. I'm worried about her being lonely."

I feel guilty for bringing it up; it would never occur to me to worry about Jay being lonely.

I follow Noah into the TV room, where Claudia sits ensconced on a lime-green couch like a kindergartner who's built her own fort from cushions. She has all the modern comforts—a remote control, snack food, a half-read magazine, and full-purpose climate control. She looks miserable in her attempt to hide how miserable she feels.

"What do you want?" she asks with her normal hostility.

"Just want to plan the evening's entertainment. Would you like to go out?"

"Do I look like I want to go out?"

"Then how 'bout pizza and a rental?"

"Fine."

"Are you sure?"

"I said 'fine.' What more do you want from me?"

Now, if this were *my* sister talking, I would say something like, *I want you to stop being such a glum diva.* But Noah is clearly a better (or, at the very least, a more patient) person than I am, since he takes it all in stride.

"One pizza and one rental coming up!" he says cheerily. "We'll be back soon." Claudia doesn't respond. She just turns the TV up louder.

"Exit . . . stage right," Noah says to me. We barrel back to the kitchen.

"Is this her usual state?" I have to ask.

"Not always. Right now I think she's mad at our parents. And I think she's trying to impress you."

"Impress me?"

"Well . . . maybe *impress* isn't the right word. I think she's picked up on the fact . . . that I like you."

"And does she realize I like you back?" I ask, drifting closer, fingers moving over his shirt.

"Definitely."

"Then I must say, you have a very observant sister." We are at whisper distance now.

"Cut it out!" Claudia shouts from the other room.

Noah and I burst out laughing, which no doubt will only make her angrier. The TV is silent now, waiting for our next move.

We pick up the credit cards and head back to town.

Please Rewind Before Returning

Noah and I split up—he'll get the pizza while I get the rental. This is probably for the best, since I'm headed to Spiff's Videorama, where newbies are discouraged. Spiff is the reason most of us still have VCRs—he's a tapehead like djs are vinyl freaks. He refuses to carry DVDs or any of the new technology.

Spiff arranges the videos in his store according to his own logic. *American Pie* is filed under Action/Adventure, while *Forrest Gump* sits in Pornography along with other inspirational classics. Spiff will never, ever tell you where a tape is, or even if it's in. You have to find it for yourself or leave empty-handed. He doesn't give a damn about any of us—just the movies. This is probably why we keep coming back.

Noah has given me a brief lowdown of what Claudia is willing to watch. Basically, if it features an Indie It Girl, it's a safe bet. John Cusack is also a plus. I head to Drama to look for *Say Anything* (knowing full well that Spiff believes that comedies hold life's true drama).

"Hey, Paul."

It's my name, coming from Foreign Language. It's my name . . . and it's Kyle's voice.

I'm caught in Comedy. Only Science Fiction stands between us. It's a big section, but not big enough.

"Paul?" Kyle says again, this time hesitant. His expression is more open to me than it's been since we broke up. I mean, since he dumped me.

"Hey, Kyle."

There's nobody else in the store—just me and Kyle and Spiff at the counter, watching the monitor he devotes solely to Tarantino and Julie Andrews.

"I've been meaning to talk to you," he says. He shifts from foot to foot. I look down at the frayed cuffs above his shoes. I remember pulling a thread from those very frays and then touching the ankle underneath, all a part of a Sunday-park daydream that surprised me by actually being real.

His sneakers are different, though. I notice that.

I don't know what I'm supposed to say. I don't really want to get into a conversation right now, especially since Noah is supposed to drop by when the pizza's ready. And at the same time, I'm dying to know: What could he possibly have to tell me?

"I'm sorry," he says. So plain, so clear. I lean on the nearest rack, nearly knocking over a full collection of Abbott and Costello.

"Why?" I ask. Maybe I've misheard him. I try to think of a word that could sound like *sorry*, but there isn't a single one.

"I was wrong. I made a mistake. I hurt you. And I'm sorry." Then, as an afterthought—a punctuation—"I just had to tell you that."

How many times have I imagined this conversation? And yet, it's not at all like I pictured it would be. I thought I would be angry. I thought I would turn his *sorry* into a spiked thing to throw right back at his heart. I thought I would say, *I'll bet you're sorry* or *Not as sorry as I am for ever getting involved with you.*

I didn't think I'd feel such a lack of rage. I didn't think I'd want to tell him it was okay.

I look at *The Breakfast Club* in his hands and remember all the times we rented it, how we would take turns reciting the lines—

sometimes I'd be the jock, sometimes he'd be the geek or the princess. I know he must remember this, too. I know he couldn't rent that movie without in some way thinking of me.

"You don't have to say anything," he continues—I remember how silence makes him nervous. "You probably don't want to talk to me."

"That's not true," I find myself saying, even though the better (i.e., smaller) part of my brain is yelling, *STOP IT! STOP IT!*

"Really?"

I nod. The door to the video store opens and I jump back a few feet, practically into Romance. But it's just Seven and Eight from school, too lost in each other to care about anyone else. Seeing them makes me feel wistful.

"Are you waiting for someone?" Kyle asks, unerringly picking the one question I least want to come out of his mouth.

"Why are you doing this now?" I deflect. "A week ago, you wouldn't even look at me in the halls. What's going on?"

"Don't you get it?" For the first time, he looks a little fiery and irritated. "The reason I couldn't talk to you was because I felt so bad for not talking to you."

"That doesn't make sense," I shoot back. But of course it makes perfect sense.

Kyle goes on, his expression half desperate and half appeasing. "There was a time I thought I was right. And that's when I was the most wrong. But the past month or so—I tried to stop thinking about you, and I couldn't. I just couldn't. I don't expect you to understand, but I can't avoid it anymore. I can't avoid *you* anymore. I walk around the school and I can feel you hating me. And the worst part is, I can't blame you."

Don't make him feel better, that smaller (better) part of my brain screams. *Don't accept his apology so easi*—

"I don't hate you," I say. "I've never hated you. I was hurt."

"I know. I'm really, really sorry."

75

The door opens again, and there's Noah, hoisting the pizza box like the Dino Diner waitress in the opening credits of *The Flintstones*. Kyle catches my glance and takes a small step forward.

"You've got to go, don't you?"

I nod. And then, surprising even myself, I take *The Breakfast Club* out of his hand.

"I need a movie," I say.

"Can we talk again? Like Monday, after school?"

This is bad news. I know it's bad news. But I've got to keep on following it. I've got to see how the bad news ends.

"I'll meet you outside the chem lab. Only for a little bit."

"Thank you," Kyle says to me. And I have to fight the urge to say thank you back.

It doesn't make sense. Nothing makes sense.

"Paul?"

By the time Noah sees me, Kyle's retreated to Fitness. I walk over and Noah looks at the box in my hand.

"Good choice," he says. "That's one of Claudia's favorites."

I can feel Kyle watching us, even though I can't see him. Noah doesn't notice. He is so happy, so oblivious. As Spiff signs out the tape, I try to muster all my happiness and obliviousness back. Then, as I step through the doorway, I turn for a last look. Kyle sees me turn and raises his hand. I don't know what he's doing, then the hand moves a little back and forth. He is waving to me. It is both a good-bye and a hello.

I am so confused.

Noah is talking to me about the five Italian women who were waiting in front of him at the pizza joint, each wanting a different topping on their pizza, enraged when the toppings overlapped on a single slice. The pizza guy tried to explain that toppings are not an exact science— sometimes in the melting process a stray piece of sausage ends up snuggled next to an anchovy. The women insisted on sending the pie back.

I shake my head at the right places. I laugh at the right places. But I am not there with him. My mind is back in the video store, in one of the sections between Comedy and Drama.

I become a little wary that Noah isn't noticing my distance. Then I get more angry at myself for digressing.

As we near his house, I am able to summon up the more wonderful events of the day. Our first kiss seems like ages ago. It is already becoming a memory.

I ride the Noah train of thought—spinning into his house, dealing with Claudia's begrudging approval of the movie selection—before the movie derails me again. *What was I thinking?* Molly Ringwald makes me think of Kyle. Judd Nelson makes me think of Kyle. Even the goddamn principal makes me think of Kyle.

Stupid. Stupid. Stupid.

Then I realize something. Noah seems just as distracted. After Ally Sheedy throws her ham at the statue, I leave the room to reheat the pizza. Noah follows me.

"What's up?" I ask, scared that he's caught on to me, that he's going to boot me out for mental disloyalty.

"I have a confession to make," he says. "It's hard for me to watch that movie."

"Why?"

"The first time I went over to . . . well, Pitt's house, we watched it."

I look at his pained, solemn expression. And then I burst out laughing. Not because it's funny (although in many ways it is). Because I feel a release.

"I know *exactly* how you feel," I say, *briefly* mentioning Kyle (not by name, and not including more recent events).

The night is saved.

We stay in the kitchen for the rest of the video. Noah breaks out a Winnie the Pooh cookbook and we decide to make lemon squares.

"You two are insane," Claudia pronounces when the movie is

over and she comes into the kitchen to find us covered with powdered sugar and flour.

"Why, thank you," Noah says. I curtsy. Claudia says she's going to sleep.

Perhaps it's Claudia's presence right over our heads, but Noah and I keep our affections quiet for the rest of the night. We relish the briefest of touches—brushing against each other as we take the lemon squares out of the oven, skimming hand over hand when we reach to turn off the oven, pressing arm against arm as we wash out the mixing bowls.

His parents aren't home yet when it's time for me to leave. Tiredness has crept into our conversation.

"Meet me before the morning bell," I say, reaching up to touch his hair.

"I'll be there," he replies, ruffling me back, kissing me good-bye.

As I walk back outside, I take a deep breath. Sure, Kyle's still in the back of my mind. But I think I can manage to keep Noah in the front.

Things Unsaid

When I see Noah on Monday morning, I can tell that something has shifted within me, within him, and within us. Before, it was all about hope and anticipation. Now it's about hope, anticipation, and proximity. I want to be close to him—not out of some vague notion of what it would be like, but because I have already been close to him and I don't want that to stop.

We talk about our mornings and leave so many things unsaid: the choreography of our note passing, our happiness in seeing each other, a little of our fear, our desire to keep our displays of affection private. The first bell rings, and I'm not sure what we'll do—is there a way to acknowledge our newfound closeness without being one of those couples who can't get through the day without a loud hallway snog?

It's Noah who finds the answer, without me having to ask the question. "I'll see you later," he says, and as he does, he runs his finger briefly over my wrist. It passes over me like air, and makes me shiver like a kiss.

I walk into French class feeling very, very lucky.

"Good weekend?" Joni asks once I sit down in front of her.

"Great weekend," I reply.

"I'm sorry I didn't call you. I was with Chuck."

Of course you were.

Before she can say any more, Ms. Kaplansky begins her conjugations. We continue our conversation in folded, college-ruled form.

Chuck and I went to the driving range. I wanted to mini-golf, but he said that was for wusses. So he taught me how to swing. After a while, he started calling me his eighteenth hole. Then he took me to the nicest place for dinner, and he was so sweet about it. He tried to order us drinks, but the waitress just laughed. Chuck was steamed for a while about that, but I cheered him up. Did you go out with your lover boy?

Yes. Noah and I spent Saturday together. It was groovy. I like him a lot.

I want juicy details.

I had Tropicana for breakfast this morning. Without pulp.

That's not what I meant. Fine. Be secretive. Like I keep anything from you. By the way, Ted's started to stalk me. Chuck and I are very upset by it.

What do you mean?

I mean, he keeps calling me and dropping by my house. One time I was there with Chuck, and Chuck almost pummeled him. I mean, doesn't Ted get it? I'm through with him. *Through.*

Perhaps he's hurting. [I am thinking for a moment of Kyle]

Yes, he's hurting ME and my relationship with Chuck.

At this point, Ms. Kaplansky announces a pop quiz. We all groan and clear off our desks. Ms. Kaplansky has an uncanny habit of asking us to translate phrases into French that we would never, ever use in English.

1. *Sir, are you familiar with the works of Australian film-maker Gillian Armstrong?*
2. *He was predisposed to believe that she had a case of indigestion.*
3. *I am amazed by the size of that ostrich.*

When Ms. Kaplansky is distracted, I turn and look at Joni. I don't see any softness there. I know it's Ted and not me she's angry with. But the anger still surprises me. If I can still feel vulnerability and tenderness towards Kyle (who dumped my sorry ass), then why can't Joni feel something less than hostility towards Ted, who she's left behind?

These questions haunt me throughout the day. Noah and I pass notes between every period, little observation installments to tide us over until the next real conversation. I see Ted and he looks awful—sleepless and dressed to depress. He mumbles a near-silent hello to me, then passes like a defeated shadow. I would rather have him tease me. I would rather have him yell.

Lyssa Ling makes an announcement during homeroom that the committee sign-ups for the Dowager Dance have been posted alongside the jukebox in the cafeteria. Infinite Darlene confides in me that she was the first to sign up for my committee, and that she's already planning what to wear for the first meeting. (I assume this means I should figure out when the first meeting will be; I haven't thought that far ahead.) She spits some venom about Joni and Chuck, who she's decided to call Truck, "since the other alternative is just too obscene for a lady like myself." Later in the day, Chuck walks past me. Out of allegiance to Joni, I say hello. He doesn't acknowledge me. I turn to watch him walk away. A minute later, Joni comes bounding into his arms. He acknowledges her . . . but not as much as she is acknowledging him. She is too enthusiastic to notice. Or perhaps I'm reading him wrong.

I don't encounter Kyle until our planned meeting in the chem lab after school. When I told Noah I would be meeting him thirty minutes later than usual, he didn't even ask me why. I feel guilty, both because of the truth I didn't volunteer and because I know that if I had been in his place, I would've asked.

Kyle and I sit at one of the chem tables; the words of our conversation will fall from the air into empty glass beakers, awaiting invisible measure. Behind Kyle, the equation-strewn board hangs like cryptic wallpaper. Neither Kyle nor I take chemistry. I figured this would be neutral ground.

I study his face—the close-cropped black hair, the scatter-freckles, the shadow-hint stubble. He looks different than when I last really knew him. His features have lost some fierceness. His angles are not so sure of themselves.

"I'm sorry for springing that on you in the video store," he begins, his voice steady and low. "That's not how I'd planned it to be."

"How did you plan it to be?" I ask, not to be snarky but because I am genuinely curious.

"I planned it to be a million different things," he replies. "And in the end, I couldn't figure which one it should be."

"But now you've told me." Part of me is still expecting him to take it all back, for this to be his one last cruel trick on my mind.

He nods.

"And what do you want from me?" I ask.

"I don't know." He looks me right in the eye for a moment, then looks behind me, to the periodic table of the elements. "I know I don't have any right to do this. I was really . . . I don't know what the word is for what I was to you. I didn't break up with you the right way. Something inside me flipped out and I . . . I couldn't stand you. It wasn't your fault. But I couldn't stand you. I needed to . . . I needed to obliterate you. Not you personally. But the thought of you. Your presence."

"Why?"

"It was just a feeling—it was an *instinct*. I had to do it. It wasn't right. It didn't feel right."

"But you didn't have to lash out at me," I say, my voice rising until I bring it back down. "You could have just told me. Said 'it doesn't feel right.' "

"No"—he's looking at me again now—"you don't understand. You would've talked me out of it. I would've backed down."

"Maybe you would've backed down because you didn't really want to do it."

"You see—you would've used that logic on me. And I didn't want to use your logic."

"So instead you *obliterate* me?"

He's playing with one of the beakers now, looking at it in his hand. "I know—I'm sorry."

I decide to continue the narrative. "So you dump me. You bad-mouth me. Then a couple of weeks later you're in the halls playing tonsil hockey with Mary Anne McAllister, telling everyone that I'd tricked you into liking guys. Now what? It didn't work with Mary Anne or Cyndi or Joanne or whoever else, and you've decided to come back to my side again?"

"It's not like that."

"Then what is it like?" I can see he's confused, I can see he's trying to tell me something. But all of my own hurt is coming out now—and it's *angry* hurt. "Please tell me what it's like. Because as you've been walking past me all these months—as everyone has been asking me, 'Whatever happened with Kyle?' and I've been trying to piece together your side of the story from all the second-hand accounts I've heard—all this time, I have been wondering more than anything else *what you think it's like.*"

He starts to shiver then. And I remember it so clearly—how he used to shiver when he was upset, when he was overwhelmed. There was nothing he or I could do to make it stop. When he told me his brother had learned he had diabetes, when his father yelled at him on a Sunday visit for quitting basketball, when we got to the ending of *Boys Don't Cry*—these were the only times I got to hold him with all my strength, as his body shook out what his mind couldn't handle. After the first time, when he'd tried to laugh the whole thing off, we hadn't talked about it. We just rode it out, until I wasn't there anymore.

I want to touch him right now. Not hold him, just touch him. But I'm paralyzed. My own reaction to being overwhelmed.

"I'm sorry," he mutters.

"Don't be. I'm sorry I snapped at you."

"No." He looks at me again; the shivering subsides. "I know you hate me. You have every right to hate me. You don't have to speak to me again."

He gets up to leave, and my paralysis is broken. I put my hand on his arm and gesture to him to sit down.

"Listen to me, Kyle," I say. He sits back down and angles his face toward mine. "I mean this entirely. And I'll only say it once. I do not hate you, and have never hated you. I was angry at you and depressed by you and confused about you. But hate never came into it."

"Thank you," he whispers.

I continue quietly. "If you want me to forgive you, I guess I have. If you want to know that I don't hate you, you know that now. Is that all?"

A slight shiver again.

"No," he says.

"What, then?" I ask gently.

"I need your help, Paul. I have no right to ask you for it, but I can't think of anyone else to talk to."

I am already involved. I've put myself in this position, and the truth is that I don't really mind.

"What is it, Kyle?"

"I'm so confused."

"Why?"

"I still like girls."

"So?"

"And I also like guys."

I touch his knee. "It doesn't sound like you're confused, then."

"But I wanted to be one or the other. With you, I wanted just to like you. Then, after you, I wanted to just like the girls. But every time I'm with one, I think the other's possible."

"So you're bisexual."

Kyle's face flushes. "I hate that word," he tells me, slumping back in his chair. "It makes it sound like I'm divided."

"When really you're doubled?"

"Right-O."

I smile. It's been a long time since I've heard a *Right-O*.

I know some people think liking both guys and girls is a cop-out. Some of Infinite Darlene's biggest rivals save their deepest scorn for the people they call "dabblers." But I think they're totally full of garbage. I don't see why, if I'm wired to like guys, someone else can't be wired to like both girls and guys.

"We could call you an ambisexual. A duosexual. A—"

"Do I really have to find a word for it?" Kyle interrupts. "Can't it just be what it is?"

"Of course," I say, even though in the bigger world I'm not so sure. The world loves stupid labels. I wish we got to choose our own.

We pause for a moment. I wonder if that's all—if he just needed to say the truth and have it heard. But then Kyle looks at me with unsure eyes and says, "You see, I don't know who I'm supposed to be."

"Nobody does," I assure him.

He nods. I see there is something else he wants to say. But he keeps it inside, and it fades somewhere behind his expression.

"Do you think we can be friends?" he asks.

It's so funny—if he had asked that during the break-up, that old "we'll be friends" fallback, I would have laughed out loud or torn out all his hair. But now, here, it actually works. It means exactly what it says.

"Yes," I answer. Then he surprises me. He leans out of his chair and envelops me in a hug. This time he holds me with all his strength, even though I don't shiver. I don't know what to do at all.

I know he wants me to feel like comfort. And deep in my heart, I know I am afraid that he'll feel like comfort, too.

Pinball

I tell Joni everything.

Then she tells Chuck.

A few days pass between the events of these two sentences. But the effect is the same.

I find out from Infinite Darlene. This alone means trouble, since Infinite Darlene tries to put as many degrees of separation as possible between herself and Chuck.

"Oh, honey," she says, "they were talking about it in the locker room."

"Talking about what?" I ask.

And she tells me: They were talking about me and Kyle, and me and Noah.

Then it gets worse.

"I'm only telling you for your own good," Infinite Darlene murmurs under her breath. "Rip is in on it."

Rip is our resident oddsmaker. His parents own islands, so his allowance allows him to bet on just about anything: How many times will the principal's secretary use the word *the* in the morning announcements? How many kids will pass by classroom 303 between sixth and seventh periods? What color will Trilby Pope wear the most in the month of April? Rip is ready to make the odds and stand by them.

He loves betting on how long couples will last.

"What are my odds?" I ask.

Infinite Darlene pouts a little at me. "Darlin', you don't want to know that, do you?"

"I'm serious."

Infinite Darlene sighs. "It's six to one that you end up with Noah, five to one that you end up back with Kyle, and two to one that you botch both chances and end up alone in the next twenty days."

"Which did you bet on?"

Infinite Darlene flutters her eyelashes at me. "A girl never tells," she chirps. Then she spirits herself away.

I wonder what the odds are that Noah has heard the gossip. Two to one? Even?

I haven't noticed any change in his heart, any sudden suspicion or wariness. And I've been seeing him a lot the past week. We've been *dating*. On Wednesday we sneaked into the city after school, to go to a museum free night and look at all the people there. The art students stood like intellectual twigs in worn-through sweaters, while the too-beautiful Europeans dipped and glided around them, conversing in languages both floral and spicy. On Thursday we hung out with Tony. It felt like ages since I'd last seen him. Noah and Tony seemed to get along pretty okay, although Noah's presence did complicate the homework routine.

We've also been kissing like crazy. Hours pass and we don't notice. We have all the time in the world because it feels like, for once, the world is giving us the time we need.

Luckily, I haven't had to disappear from everyone else's lives in order to be a part of Noah's. We don't want to be that kind of couple (see: Joni and Chuck). I've also had time to check in with Kyle, for shorter amounts of time. It's hard to resist the pull of someone who needs you. We've kept all of our exchanges limited to conversation—but the fact that we're having conversations at all means something. Neither of us knows what.

I find myself relieved that both Noah and Kyle are going away for the weekend—Noah to hang with his old-town friends, Kyle to visit an ailing aunt.

Joni makes the mistake of approaching me on Friday afternoon, after I've talked to Infinite Darlene. Chuck is at her side. The fact that she doesn't realize I know she blabbed is more amazing than the fact that I didn't know in the first place.

"We're going to pick up Tony," she says. "Wanna come?"

These are perhaps the only words in the world that could get me into a car with her at this point. She appeals to the part of me that yearns for instant time travel—a trip to the not-so-long-ago, when Tony, Joni, and I were a band of three.

Of course, this time Chuck comes along. He doesn't offer me the front seat. He takes it as if it's rightfully his.

Joni doesn't seem to notice.

So I sit in the backseat amidst the empty Fresh Samantha bottles (hers) and smashed Pepsi cans (his). I wonder when Joni stopped recycling in a prompt manner, and start to regret my voluntary passengerdom. The anger I feel towards Joni for sharing my thoughts with Chuck begins to reach the boiling point again. I vow to talk to her at the first moment I can catch her without him.

That moment never comes. They don't even take bathroom breaks from each other.

My testiness is a little offset once Tony jumps into the backseat with me; now I have someone to share glances with. The first glance—me wide-eyed, Tony's eyebrow raised—comes when Chuck hijacks the radio and blasts some Testosterone Rock, the kind of music best suited for "professional" wrestling compilations. The second glance—me squinting in disbelief, Tony looking to heaven—is prompted when Chuck starts to sing along and chastises us for not joining in. As if I know the lyrics to a song called "She's All Mouth."

Joni doesn't sing along, either, but she makes a lame attempt at drumming on the steering wheel. At one point, she accidentally hits the horn, which cracks Chuck up.

"Nice toots," he chuckles.

Third glance—me and Tony each pleading, *Get us out of this car now.*

We head to the local diner, the kind of place where you need a mob connection in order to get your song on the jukebox. The waitresses are perfectly lacquered, the waiters freshly slicked. The menu is the size of a wood plank and takes as long to read as the morning paper. Breakfast is always served, most of the time as dinner.

As we sit down in a booth, I see Joni's eyes briefly flash worry. It's the first non–Chuck-related reaction she's had since I got into her car. Or at least that's what I think at first. Soon I realize that all her reactions are Chuck-related in some way.

I turn and follow her gaze. I see Ted sitting three tables away with Jasmine Gupta. His back is to me, but when Jasmine sees me looking, she winks.

Kyle could take lessons from Jasmine—she'll fall for anybody, guy or girl. The hitch is that the person has to be on the rebound from a serious break-up. Something about this fragile-yet-vindictive state entrances her.

The old Joni comes back to us for a brief moment.

"I see Ted's finally gone the predictable route," she snarks. (In all his other break-ups with Joni, he had chosen not to flee in Jasmine's direction.)

"He's scum," Chuck mutters, perhaps because he thinks it's his duty to do so.

"No, he's not," I say pleasantly.

"What's everybody getting to eat?" Tony interjects. One of the weaknesses of being mellow is an inability to deal with non-mellow moments.

"I bet Joni'll get the grilled swiss," Chuck says with a smile.

"He knows me so well!" Joni replies. I wonder whether that's really what she'd planned to order.

What have you done with the old Joni, you imposter?!

"That sounds good," Tony says. Our waitress arrives and we are freed from one another's conversation for a minute or two. After she leaves, we stick to non-controversial topics like school and homework. It is all terribly boring, which is not something our diner excursions used to be.

Of course, I blame Chuck. And Joni, for being with Chuck.

I can see her trying to watch Ted without appearing to watch Ted. I know she can read the back of his head like the rest of us can read a facial expression.

We make it through the meal. Tony becomes voluble about a church retreat his parents are threatening to send him on.

"That's just plain wrong," Chuck declares, spearing a french fry.

After we finish eating, we head to the pinball machines at the back of the diner. Let me tell you — nothing can compare to putting the entirety of your fate in a small metal sphere that bounces across light, sound, and plastic. The machines still only cost a quarter, and each of us has our superstitions. I always play best when I use a Georgia or Rhode Island quarter. Tony is partial to Pennsylvania and Maryland. Ted, I know, has a stack of Connecticuts in a drawer at home; sometimes we swap in the cafeteria to build our own caches.

Tony and I always take turns off the same machine, decked out in gold lights and Elvis. It plays "Love Me Tender" if you break 10,000. "Can't Help Falling in Love" greets you at 25,000. A losing shot ends with "Heartbreak Hotel."

Chuck commandeers his own machine — sometimes he splits

flippers with Joni, sometimes he chooses to go it alone, with her cheering him on.

About fifteen minutes after we start playing, Ted and Jasmine come over.

"What are you gay boys doing?" he asks me and Tony.

"Who are you calling a gay boy, loser?" Chuck shouts out.

"Uh, Chuck?" I say. "He was talking to me. And Tony."

"Oh."

But Ted isn't going to let it pass. He slaps a Connecticut quarter onto Chuck's machine.

"I got next game," he says. "You better make this one good."

Since it's Tony's turn on Elvis, I fade back a little. As Ted hawk-eyes Chuck's game, Jasmine steps beside me.

"What are you up to?" I ask her.

She smiles flirtatiously. "Who says I'm up to anything?"

Jasmine has always been a little bit after me, if only because she knows I'll never go for her.

"Are you and Ted a thing now?"

"Hardly. He just needs someone to talk to. He doesn't need any-one to talk *about*—he's already got that."

We both look over and see him glaring at Chuck and Joni. Chuck is clearly uncomfortable with this, but he doesn't know how to handle it without looking like a brute (which clearly won't go over well with this crowd). He plays a tense game of pinball. And as anybody knows, a tense game of pinball is a *doomed* game of pinball. He barely hits 8,000 before guttering out his last shot. He looks a little stunned at the score, then moves to the side of the machine so Ted can get his play.

I already know Ted is going to win. He's damn good at pinball. And he wants it bad.

Joni looks like she's waiting for someone to pull an alarm. She knows what's going to happen, too. She puts her hand on Chuck's shoulder, already near the comforting zone.

Ted sees this and plays harder. Tony's game ends at a respectable 16,749. It's my turn, but I don't move. We're all watching Ted now.

Usually Ted's a yeller, shouting at the ball to hook left or bounce right. Now, though, he has a Zen-like calm. A casual observer might say that he has become one with the ball, that he has made himself the ball.

But I know the truth.

Chuck is the ball.

And Ted plans to wham the heck out of it.

Bumper to bumper, save after save—the numbers escalate. Six thousand. Seven thousand. Chuck leans in from the side and looks at the score.

We may never know whether it's the lean that does it or whether it's Ted's reaction to the lean that causes the ball to angle a little into the narrow alley between the flippers. Ted's opinion is loud and clear.

"You tilted me!" he shouts, slamming one hand on the pinball machine and poking the other one at Chuck.

"It was all your fault, buddy," Chuck shouts back. He knocks Ted's hand away from him.

"Don't do this," Joni says.

"Stay out of it," Chuck snaps.

"Don't tell her what she can or can't do!" Ted argues.

Chuck shoves Ted away from the machine. Ted pushes back and knocks Chuck's baseball cap off his head.

Then Tony steps in between them and starts singing "If I Had a Hammer" at the top of his lungs.

I can't believe it. I once told him that the best way to break up a fight is to step between the two people and start singing ancient folk songs. But I'd never heard of anyone actually doing such a thing.

It works. As Tony's voice cracks, hammering out justice and warning and love between the brothers and the sisters all over this land, Ted and Chuck back off. Joni grabs Chuck's arm and pulls him away from the pinball area. After a beat, Jasmine does the same with Ted, wrapping her arm around him only after Joni turns back to look.

"Nice job," I tell Tony.

"It was either that or 'Michael, Row the Boat Ashore.' "

We look at the couples in our midst and decide it's time to take a break from everyone else.

Tomorrow we'll hit the mountain.

Hitting the Mountain

Tony and I figure the best thing a straight boy with religious, intolerant parents can do for his love life is tell his parents he's gay. Before Tony's parents discovered he was gay, they wouldn't let him shake hands with a girl. Now if he mentions he's doing something with a girl—any girl—they practically pimp him out the door.

Jay and I wait in a Laundromat parking lot a couple of blocks from Tony's house. Tony tells his parents that he's going on an outing with Mary Catherine Elizabeth from school. The 'rents immediately have visions of Immaculate Connections and press spending cash into Tony's hands. He leaves his house dressed for repressed flirtation. When he gets to the car, I throw him a duffel and he changes into some hiking gear. Jay drops us off at the local water supply reservation and we hit the mountain.

It's not a mountain, really. Not in a Rockies or Appalachian sense. Any serious mountain climber would call it a hill. But Tony and I aren't serious mountain climbers. We're suburban teen gay boys who need a place with nature and walking paths. I relish the anonymity of the trees. I've been here so many times that I don't mind when I'm lost.

I first came here with Tony. It's his place, really. We'd been hanging around for a few weeks by then, grabbing movies and surfing the mall. He told me there was a place he wanted to show me, so one Friday after school I hopped over to his house and we walked an hour to get to this reservation. I had passed it a million times before, but I'd never been inside.

Tony knows the names of trees and birds. As we walk around, he points them out to me. I try to record them in my mind, but the information never holds. What matters to me is the emotional meaning of the objects. I still remember which rock we talked on the first time we came here. I always salute the tree I tried to climb on our fourth visit—and ended up nearly breaking my neck on. And then there's the clearing.

Tony didn't explain it to me right away. On our second or third visit, he pointed through a thatch of trees and said, "There's a clearing in there." A few times later, we poked our heads inside—sure enough, there was a patch of grass about the size of two trailers, guarded on all sides by branches, trunks, and leaves. It wasn't until we'd been coming to the mountain for a month or two that Tony told me that he'd lived in the clearing for a week—the week after his parents found out he was gay. His mother had decided to swap his winter clothes for his summer clothes and went through his drawers while he was at school. She found a magazine folded into a flannel shirt—nothing raunchy, just an old issue of *The Advocate* that Tony had bought on one of his city trips. At first she didn't understand—she thought *The Advocate* sounded like something a lawyer would read. Then she sat on his bed, opened up to the table of contents, and Tony's secret wasn't a secret anymore.

They didn't kick Tony out of the house, but they made him want to leave. They didn't yell at him—instead they prayed loudly, delivering all of their disappointment and rage and guilt to him in the form of an address to God. This was before he knew me, before he knew anyone who would take him in and tell him he was all right. So he kipped together a tent and some clothes and pitched his life in the clearing. He still went to school and let his parents know he was okay. Eventually, they reached a collect-call truce. He went back home and they promised to hold back their condemnation. Their prayers were quieter, but they still filled the air. Tony couldn't trust them any longer—not with the gay part of his life. Now he keeps the few love notes he's ever received in a box at Joni's house, and borrows my magazines instead of buying his own. He can only do e-mail at school or a friend's house; his family's computer now screens its sites.

I know Tony still goes to the clearing every now and then, to think or to dream. I give it a silent salute every time we pass. We never sit down there together. I don't want to trespass on his solitude—I want to be around when he chooses to step out of it.

"How are things with Noah?" he asks me now, as we set off on our hike. As usual, we have the path to ourselves.

"Good. I miss him."

"Do you wish he was here now?"

"No."

"Good."

We walk a few more steps, then Tony asks, "So how are things with Kyle?" I love Tony dearly because there's no judgment in this question.

"I don't know what's going on," I tell him. "He loved me, then he loved me not. Now he needs me. I'm sure pretty soon he'll need me not."

We walk along for a few minutes in silence. I know Tony hasn't lost the subject, though.

"Are you sure that's healthy?" he asks at last.

"I think it's good he's opening up," I say.

"I don't mean for him. I mean for you."

I'm confused. "He's the one asking for help. Why would it be unhealthy for me?"

Tony shrugs.

"The thing is, I'm not vulnerable this time," I explain. "It doesn't mean everything to me."

"Did you know you were vulnerable last time?"

This one I can answer in confidence. "Yes. Of course. That's what falling in love is all about."

Tony sighs. "I wouldn't know."

The part of me that misses Noah right now has an equal part in Tony. The difference is that his longing doesn't have a name or a face.

"Someday your prince will come," I assure him.

"And the first thing I'm going to say to him is, 'What took you so long?'"

We reach the mountain's steepest incline. We pick up fallen branches to use as walking sticks—not because we really need them, but because it's more fun to walk that way. We start talking in our own language (*"Sasquan helder figglebarth?" "Yeh sesta." "Cumpsy!"*), then stop when Tony hears a birdcall that interests him greatly. (The only birdcall I know is the Road Runner's *BEEP BEEP.*)

Tony's sights alight on the highest branches. I can't see a thing, but after a moment, he looks very pleased.

"A bohunk. Not native to this area. But that makes it more mysterious."

I nod. I can go for mysterious.

We continue walking.

"So what's up with you?" I ask.

"Not much."

"And how are things?"

"Fine."

RRRRRRRR. I make a loud game-show-buzzer noise. "I'm sorry," I say, "we don't recognize 'fine' as an acceptable answer. We see it as a conversational cop-out. So please, try again."

Tony sighs again, but not that heavily. He knows he's been snagged. If I ever say "fine" to him, he reacts the same way.

"I've actually been thinking about life lately, and this one image keeps coming to me," he says. "Do you know when you cross against traffic? You look down the street and see a car coming, but you know you can get across before it gets to you. So even though there's a DON'T WALK sign, you cross anyway. And there's always a split second when you turn and see that car coming, and you know that if you don't continue moving, it will all be over. That's how I feel a lot of the time. I know I'll make it across. I always make it across. But the car is always there, and I always stop to watch it coming."

He gives me a low smile. "You know, sometimes I wish I had your life. But I'm sure I wouldn't be much good at it."

"I'm not that great at it myself."

"You get by."

"So do you."

"I try."

I find myself thinking back to something I saw on the local news about a year ago. A teen football player had died in a car accident. The cameras showed all his friends after the funeral—these big hulking guys, all in tears, saying, "I loved him. We all loved him so much." I started crying, too, and I wondered if these guys had told the football player they loved him while he was alive, or whether it was only with death that this strange word, *love,* could be used. I vowed then and there that I would never hesitate to speak up to the people I loved. They deserved to know they gave meaning to my life. They deserved to know I thought the world of them.

"You know I love you," I say to Tony now, not for the first time. "You are really one of the greatest people I know."

Tony can't take a compliment, and here I am, giving him the best one I can give. He brushes it off, sweeping his hand to the side. But I know he's heard it. I know he knows it.

"I'm glad we're here," he says.

We switch to another language—not our invented language or

the language we've learned from our lives. As we walk further into the woods and up the mountain, we speak the language of silence. This language gives us space to think and move. We can be both here and elsewhere at the same time.

I hit the peak with Tony and then we turn back around. I am conscious of this in my silence, but I am also conscious of Noah and Kyle at their different destinations, miles away. I am conscious of Joni, who is no doubt somewhere with Chuck, not getting any silence unless he permits it. (Is this an unfair thought? I'm truly not sure.)

I don't know where Tony is while he's with me—maybe he's simply concentrating on the birdcalls and the slant of the sunlight, which hits through the trees in a pattern that decorates his arm with the space between leaves.

But maybe it's more than that. As we get back to the main path, Tony turns to me and asks for a hug.

Now, I don't believe in doing hugs halfway. I can't stand people who try to hug without touching. A hug should be a full embrace— as I wrap my arms around Tony, I am not just holding him, but also trying to lift off his troubles for a moment so that the only thing he can feel is my presence, my support. He accepts this embrace and hugs me back. Then his posture raises an alarm—his back straightens out of the hug, his hands fall a little.

I look at his face and realize that he's seen something behind me. I let go of him and turn to find two adults gawking.

"Tony?" the woman asks.

But she doesn't really need to ask. She knows it's Tony.

After all, she's his mother's best friend.

Everybody Freaks Out

Tony is grounded, and his mom's best friend can't keep her mouth shut. The church group network goes into overtime, and by the time I get to school on Monday, I find out that Rip's odds on my love life are now twelve to one for me and Noah, ten to one for me and Kyle, eight to one for me and Tony, and one to two for me botching everything up and spending the rest of my life unrequited.

By the end of the day, the odds have changed even further, and I'm a total basket case.

It's no use protesting to people that Tony and I are just friends (only the people who know us believe me, and all the rest want to believe the opposite because it's a better story). I can't even talk to Tony anymore—I tried on Sunday but his mom hung up on me, muttering something about the devil's influence, which I think was a little overstated.

"Do you think I'm an agent of the devil?" I ask Lyssa Ling after she briefs me on Rip's odds and hands me my Dowager's Dance committee list.

"I would hope that an agent of the devil would be more attractive than you," Lyssa zings back.

Before I take offense, I look at the committee list . . . and gulp.

"Um, Lyssa? You've put both Trilby Pope and Infinite Darlene on my committee?"

"So? It's already posted. A done deal."

"Clearly, you don't realize the implications of this. They both HATE EACH OTHER'S GUTS. They can't be on my committee together."

"They both wanted to architect, and I'm not going to be the one to play favorites. They'll just have to deal. And so will you."

With that, she pulls her clipboard back to her chest and walks away.

I've gotten to school early to find Noah and see how his weekend went. But before I can find Noah, Kyle finds me.

"We have to talk," he says urgently.

"How about after school?" I ask.

"No. Right now."

As Kyle drags me into the janitor's closet, I can see the whole school watching through the eyes of the few people in the hall. I can only imagine what they're thinking, and what they'll say.

The janitor's closet has the usual brooms, mops, and buckets. At its center, though, is a state-of-the-art computer. Our janitorial staff is one of the richest in the country because of their day-trading skills. They could have retired long ago, but they all have a compulsion to clean schools.

"What is it?" I ask Kyle, trying to ignore the stock ticker scrolling across the computer screen.

Some of the confusion has lifted from his face, replaced by this decisive urgency. He doesn't look sad or happy. He looks as emotionless as a fact.

"My aunt died this weekend," he says, "and I decided that we should be together."

Before I can say anything, he continues.

"She wasn't very old, only a few years older than my mom. She always lived far away, so I didn't really know her until she moved out here for treatment. Her husband was with her; they got married two days after she got her diagnosis. He vowed he would never leave her side, and he didn't. I don't know how to describe it. She could be retching or shaking or not really there, and he would kneel right beside her, look her right in the eye, and say, 'I'm here.' And the way he said it—'I'm here'—was an 'I love you' and a 'Hang in there' and an 'I'll do anything, absolutely anything'—all these intense feelings in this one calm phrase. If he had to leave the room, he made sure she had this teddy bear propped up next to her—they called him Quincy—to take his place. Toward the end, there were these few moments when she got all anxious a few minutes after he left the room, and he would come right back in, as if he knew exactly how she felt. I came to the room early on Saturday and I saw him curled up in the hospital bed, singing Beatles songs to her and looking her in the eye. I couldn't go inside. I just stood in the doorway crying, because it was so sad and it was so beautiful.

"That night I stayed awake thinking about things. I thought about all the stupid things I've done, and you were at the top of the list. You gave me something, Paul. And I don't think I realized it until I saw Tom with my aunt Maura. Then I knew. I knew what I wanted."

He sees my expression and laughs, which makes it worse, because I like him more for it. "Don't worry," he says. "I'm not asking you to marry me, or to curl up with me in a hospital bed. I don't know what I'm asking you. All I know is this: I want something *real*. I know I'm young, and I know 'real' doesn't mean forever, like it did for Tom and Aunt Maura. But I want to feel like life matters. I had something real with you, but then the realness scared me. I decided to go for other things instead."

"Like Mary Anne McAllister?"

"Look, I freaked out on you. And now I'm freaking out about it. I'm a mess. Aunt Maura died last night, as we were driving back.

I have to go to the funeral tomorrow morning. It's going to be the worst thing. And I . . . I don't know. I wanted to talk to you before that."

What can I say to him? I think about him standing in that hospital doorway—*it was so sad and it was so beautiful*. Because, yes, I see it: Right now, tears in his eyes, not yet released, Kyle is so sad and so beautiful.

He needs me.

I know I must step to him. He won't step to me. I open my arms and he folds himself inside. I hold him as he shivers. I stroke his hair. I whisper caring words. Then he pulls his face back, tears now released, and I kiss him. Just once, so I can take some of the tears away. Just once, because I want him to know something. *I'm here*.

We hold each other again, and I can feel the moment drain from us. We are transitioning to the moment when we have to open the door and head to class. What we have right now is real, but it is an isolated reality. It is the reality of a moment, of a separate calm. When we open the door, life will resume. We will be confused once more.

I know Kyle will not ask anything else of me. I know I have taken some of his freak-out and made it my own.

Even in the janitor's closet, the bell for first period rings. Kyle wipes his face with his shirtfront—not the most delicate of gestures—and picks up his book bag.

"Thanks," he says.

"No problem," I say, and immediately regret my choice of words.

Once in the halls, we go our separate ways. I don't have time now to find Noah. Part of me is relieved.

I expect to see him after first period, by which time I've managed to turn the moment with Kyle into a dreamlike surreality, to the point that I can pretend it didn't really happen. I have a note in my hand for Noah, but he never shows up to pick it up.

Bad timing, I figure. After second period, I head straight to the classroom he's coming from. But he's not waiting for me there, either. And while an hour and a half ago I was somewhat happy to avoid him, now I'm somewhat worried that he's avoiding *me*.

At the next break, I head to the fourth-period class he's going to instead of the third-period class he's coming from. Sure enough, our paths cross. He *seems* happy to see me, but I'm not sure he *is* happy to see me. He takes my note and says we should "touch base" at lunch.

He doesn't have a note for me in return.

I stress about this on my way to lunch, also wondering what Kyle's reaction will be if I see him again. As I head distractedly to the cafeteria, I am waylaid by Infinite Darlene.

"I *must* talk to you right this moment—I am *outraged*!" she exclaims.

Here it comes, I think. Infinite Darlene has no doubt heard she's on the same committee as Trilby Pope. And she is no doubt aggrieved.

"It's not my fault," I say defensively.

"How could it be?" Infinite Darlene asks, shooting me a tilted look. "You had nothing to do with Truck kidnapping Joni's heart. And now all my fears have been realized. He is an awful, awful, sub-human being."

"What are you telling me?" I ask her.

"My goodness, haven't you heard? Truck and I had something of an altercation yesterday, and I'm afraid the truth came out." Infinite Darlene pauses dramatically. Then, seeing that I'm still in the dark, she resumes. "It was on the bus ride home from our game in Passaic. He was brooding like a pit bull because he felt I'd called the wrong plays. Please note that we won the game anyway, but that's beside the point. I said something that set him off—I honestly can't recall what it was—and he said something like, 'Well, maybe we would have scored more if you'd made more passes my way,' and I shot back, 'Honey, you *know* I'm not going to be making any passes your way.' This evil grin popped onto his face and he said, 'Well, I'm scoring anyway, and there's nothing you can do to stop it.' I said, 'So is *that* why you're doing this?' He grinned even wider. His eyes were pure spite. And I knew. That's what this is all about. Not Joni. Not love. He's getting back at me. He's going to hurt one of my friends, and it will be my fault unless I stop it. He hates us, Paul. Make no mistake."

Even for Infinite Darlene, this seems a little far-fetched. "Don't you think Joni could see through him if he was really doing this out of spite?"

Infinite Darlene puts a hand on my shoulder and looks me deep in the eye. "C'mon, Paul," she says. "We all know love makes you do stupid things."

This close, I can see through all her layers. Beneath the mascara and the lipstick and the chicken pox scar on her lower lip, beneath the girl and the boy to the person within, who is concerned and confused and sincere. I wonder if she can see through my layers as well, right through my badly held peace to all of the love confusion underneath. There's no way she can know I kissed Kyle unless she sees it in my face. I wonder if my freak-out is as legible as hers.

"We have to do something," she says. "We have to stop him."

"How?"

"I don't know. First and foremost, you have to talk to Joni."

I knew this was coming.

"You want me to tell her that the only reason Chuck is going out with her is to get back at you?"

"Not in those exact words, but yes."

"And you think she'll listen to me?"

"Honey, if she's stopped listening to you, then that's a bigger problem than anything else."

I know this much is true.

"Fine," I say. I expect Infinite Darlene to be relieved by this, but she doesn't look relieved.

"They're over there," she says, pointing to Joni and Chuck in the cafeteria, somehow eating and snuggling at the same time. "Now's as good a time as any."

Naturally, I want to look for Noah (don't I?), but I can't find a way to say no to Infinite Darlene. I head over to Joni under her watchful eye.

Joni doesn't even detach herself from Chuck when I come into range. She lets him put his hand in her back pocket. I fight the urge to *ewww*.

"What's up?" she asks. She sounds defensive, so the *ewww* must be noticeable.

"Can we talk?"

"Sure." She doesn't move.

"I mean, somewhere else."

She looks at Chuck, who's looking at me.

"We can talk here, can't we?" she says, turning back in my direction.

"No."

It's such a simple word—*no*. But it has the force of a slam. I am not going to talk to Joni in front of Chuck because that's not what I came over here to do. And Joni's not going to budge. I know this already. And that sound you hear—that *no*, that slam—is the sound of our friendship taking on the tone of a war.

"Why can't we talk here?"

"Because I want to talk to you alone."

"Well, you can't now. I'm busy."

Busy with Chuck's hand in her back pocket, and him stuffing french fries into his face, possibly thinking that his revenge against Infinite Darlene is working perfectly.

"Sorry to bother you, then," I say, hoping to thrust one last dagger of guilt her way. I turn away abruptly because I'm too afraid to see if I got the reaction I wanted.

I can't find Noah anywhere in the cafeteria. I really want to see him now. I ask around, and Eight tells me she saw him out by the soccer field with his camera. I immediately head in that direction.

He is exactly where Eight said he'd be. He is on the edge of the field, in the space between the goal line and the surrounding woods. His camera is held to his eye, his posture silently observant. I am walking up behind him, but I cannot figure out what he is taking a picture of. I see an empty set of bleachers with a half-full garbage can at its side, nothing more.

There is a faint click, then another. I circle around into Noah's side view. I look at his haphazard hair and his blue hooded sweatshirt and I realize how much I've missed him. More than touching him or kissing him, I just want to talk to him.

I feel like the Paul who kissed Kyle is a totally different person from the Paul who likes Noah. And right now, I am entirely the Paul who likes Noah. The other Paul is in another country.

"Hey," I say. He turns to me with the camera still to his eye. He doesn't smile or say anything back. He maintains his concentration, seeing me through the viewfinder.

I walk closer, until I can see myself reflected in the glass of the lens.

"Everyone's freaking out," I continue. "*I'm* freaking out. So much is happening. God, I've missed you. I'm sorry I've been so out of range."

I hear another click. I smile after the picture has been taken.

"It's okay," he says. Then he puts the camera down and I can see his headlong expression.

"How was your weekend?" I ask.

"Good. I thought about some things." From the way he says it, I can tell that all of these things are me, and that I'm not going to like what follows.

"Like what?"

"Like . . . maybe we should slow down a little. Take a time-out."

I nod as if I understand what he's saying. But then I ask, "Why?"

"Because I need to."

"Why?"

"Because . . . I feel . . . I feel like I don't know what I feel. I really like you, but I'm not sure what that means. I don't know what you want from me. And I don't know if I can give it to you. I went home this weekend and I thought about all these things. I was talking to my old friends about you, and about me, and hearing it all out loud I realized that I've gotten myself into something that I might not be ready for. I mean, I know you're not going to hurt me, but at the same time I don't want to throw myself into a place where I can be hurt. Chloe, Angela, and Jen pointed that out to me, and I can see where they're coming from."

The bottom line is clear to me. "You're freaking out," I say.

He smiles a little at that. "Maybe. But I need to sort this out. And I can't be with you while I'm doing that."

"You're overanalyzing it," I argue. In the back of my mind, I'm thinking: *There are so many other reasons for you to break it off with me. Why this one?*

He raises the camera back to his eye.

"Don't take my picture," I say.

"Okay." He puts the camera down again.

"Do you want to do something this afternoon?"

He shakes his head. "How about Thursday?" he offers.

"Thursday," I repeat. Is there some sort of equation he's following that makes going out on Thursday okay, but not this afternoon?

I don't want to, but I sort of understand where he's coming from. *Be careful,* he's saying. I want him to be careful with me, too. And sometimes careful feels like it has to be slow. Especially if you've been with someone fast and careless before.

He looks so nervous. He *does* still like me, but it's freaking him out.

"Is that okay?" he asks, backing down a little.

"How about Tuesday?" I say.

"Wednesday." His seriousness is cracking.

"Tuesday and a half."

"Tuesday and three-quarters."

Because I can't think of what's between a half and three-quarters quickly enough, I agree to seeing him on Tuesday and three-quarters.

"I just need to think," he says.

I know I shouldn't, but I lean over and kiss him. I press against his camera, and it takes pictures of our feet as he kisses me back.

"That's definitely something to think about," he says once we pull apart. But he doesn't give in entirely.

"Tuesday and three-quarters," he says.

"Tuesday and three-quarters," I agree.

When he's gone, I miss him. I know I will miss him for the rest of today and tomorrow, and the three-quarters after. Even though he doesn't know about the Paul who kissed Kyle, even though I can't think of anything I might have said or done to make him freak out, I feel like it's all my fault. I tempted fate, and now fate is kicking me back a little.

What's worse is that I don't have anyone to talk to about it. Tony's in exile, Joni's experiencing pair-a-noia, Ted isn't a real option, and Infinite Darlene would probably tell me I'm getting what I deserve. So all the words stay contained in my head, never leaving me alone.

I space through the rest of the school day. Then Joni shoots me down to earth.

"What were you trying to pull at lunch?" she rails at me as I'm piling books back into my locker.

I notice Chuck isn't with her.

"Hey," I say, "where's your appendage?"

She slams my locker shut, narrowly missing my fingers.

"I'm sick of it, Paul," she yells. "I'm sick of your attitude and everybody else's. You want everything to stay the same. You want me to be back with Ted, and all of us to be the same little group for the rest of our little lives. But I'm not going to be like that. My world is bigger than that."

My defense mechanism kicks in. "Are you quoting Chuck directly or just paraphrasing him?" I ask, more to anger her than because I think it's true.

Bull's-eye. If my locker had popped back open, she'd be slamming it again—this time with my head in it.

"You think you're such a good friend, don't you?" she snarks. "Is that why Tony's grounded and Infinite Darlene can make you do her dirty work?"

"What are you talking about?"

"I know what she's saying about me and Chuck."

"And have you maybe paused for one clueful second to wonder if it's true? Infinite Darlene's your friend, remember?"

"She *used to be* my friend."

"Just like me, huh?"

I've pushed her to it, but still I'm startled when she says, "Just like you."

It's Kyle, of all people, who breaks in at this point.

"Hey, Paul! Hey, Joni." He bounds over and flashes me an eager look. I try to downplay it, but Joni's eyes widen a little. She's seen— I'm not sure exactly what, but it won't go unremarked upon.

I can't take it anymore. I am freaking out because I know I made a mistake with Kyle, and I am freaking out because it doesn't totally feel like a mistake. I am freaking out because my friendship with Joni is at a ten-year low, and I am freaking out because she doesn't seem to care. I am freaking out because Noah doesn't know what I want from him, and I am freaking out because I don't know what I could possibly give him in return. I am freaking out because I've been caught—not by anyone else, but by myself. I see what I am doing. And I can't stop myself from making things worse.

So I run. I make excuses and I run. Out the door. Out of the school.

But not away.

I can't make it away.

When I get home, I find a note from Noah in the front pocket of my backpack. Somehow he managed to slip it in without me noticing. Since I know I got a calculator out of the pocket after lunch, I know he got to me after I saw him. The note has only one line on it, but I'm sure it's his handwriting.

The note says:

I can't believe you kissed him.

Elsewhere

Since I was a little kid, I've been doing this thing I call Going Elsewhere. It's almost like meditation, but instead of blanking myself out, I try to color myself in. I sit in the middle of my room, on the floor, and close my eyes. I put the tunes on the stereo that will take me to the right Elsewhere. I fill myself with images. And then I watch them unwind.

My parents and even my brother are pretty cool about letting me do this. They never ask me why I need to leave. They respect my closed door. If someone calls on the phone, they tell the caller I'm Elsewhere and that I'll be back soon.

When I get home after school, the house is empty. I write a note on the pad lying on the kitchen table—*Elsewhere*—and head to my room. I put on Erasure's "Always" and take off my shoes. I sit in the exact center of the room. When I close my eyes, I begin with red.

The colors come first. Red. Orange. Aquamarine. Flashes of solid color, like origami paper lit by television light. After going through colors, I picture patterns—stripes, slants, dots. Sometimes I pass through an image in a split second. Others I hold on to. I pause on the way to Elsewhere. And then I'm there.

I never have a plan. I never know what I'm going to see after the colors and patterns are done.

This time it's a duck.

It splashes into view and beckons me forward. I see an island — your usual desert island, with crystal-blue water, perfect beach sand, and a palm tree angled in an arched slant. I pull myself ashore and lie looking at the sky. I can feel Joni pounding at a door, but I don't let her in. When I go Elsewhere, I travel alone. Shells ring my shadow. I reach over and pick one up, expecting to hear the sea. But the shells are silent. Tony walks by and waves. He looks happy, and I'm glad. I hear volcanoes in the distance, but I know I'm safe. The duck waddles at my feet. I laugh at its movements. Then it plops down into the water and begins to glide. I follow it in, wanting a swim.

I begin to sink. I am not drowning — there is no struggle, no fear. It's the opposite of floating, a simple downward fall. I am pushing through the empty water, unaware of what lies at the bottom. I expect rocks, fish, wreckage. But instead I find Noah in his studio, slashing colors into a canvas. I try to see what he's painting, but I can't. Then it occurs to me that he's not painting a picture. Instead he's painting emotions, and every color he uses means hurt. I try to swim away, but I hang suspended. This isn't Elsewhere; this is Somewhere. I try to switch back to colors and patterns, but all of them now come from Noah's brush. I try to go back to the beach, back to the volcano. But even the music in my head is telling me there's no escape. And I know this. I am floating back to the surface now. Noah grows smaller, his room diminishes. But I know it's my ultimate destination. He's where I want to be.

I don't open my eyes. Not yet. I am back now; I am sitting in the absolute center of my room, my brother's footsteps new on the stairs.

Sometimes the space between knowing what to do and actually doing it is a very short walk. Other times it is an impossible expanse. As I sit with my eyes closed, I try to gauge the distance between me and the words that I will have to say. It seems far. Very far.

I'm not ready yet.

I put my hand in my pocket and feel the edges of Noah's note. *I can't believe you kissed him.* It would be so easy to obsess about how he found out. But that's only a speculative digression. The real problem is that it's the truth.

I open my eyes. I take out my homework and do it with even less enthusiasm than usual.

I decide to call Tony. His mother answers.

"May I please speak to Tony?" I say.

"He's not here," his mother frostily answers.

"Where is he?" I ask.

She hangs up.

I call my friend Laura and am relieved to find she's not at her girlfriend's house. I ask her to call Tony and see if he's okay (I'm sure his mom will let a female caller through). She readily agrees to the assignment, and calls back fifteen minutes later to tell me he's feeling low, but the situation is survivable. His parents are keeping him under constant watch, afraid he might steal some kisses if they're not on guard. The chances of me getting to see him in the near future are about as likely as me becoming Heavyweight Champion of the World.

At dinner, my parents notice my gloom. They try to skirt around it at first, but curiosity gets the best of them, and by dessert they're plunging right in.

"What's going on?" my mother asks.

"Are you okay?" my father backs her up.

"What have you done now?" Jay chimes in.

I tell them about what happened with Tony.

"Perhaps it's time to send in the P-FLAG commandos," Jay suggests. In our town, P-FLAG (Parents and Friends of Lesbians and Gays) is as big a draw as the PTA.

My mother nods at my brother while my father shakes his head at Tony's parents.

I dash back up to my room before I start blabbing about Noah. Jay calls me on it anyway.

"Busy day?" he pokes his head in and asks.

"How'd you bet?" I ask, since I know he must've heard things from Rip.

"I didn't," he says, and holds on for a second. "Just do me a favor and tip me off when you know which way it's going to go."

"I'll do that," I say.

"Hang in, Paul." He closes the door gently.

I try to arm myself with distractions. I finish my homework. I read a book. I go downstairs and watch TV. But the image of Elsewhere—of Noah in his studio—hasn't gone away.

I can't believe you kissed him.

It isn't until eleven that I decide I can't take it any longer. I know what I have to do.

My parents are in their bedroom, watching a cop show on cable.

"I have to go out," I tell them. "I know it's late and I know you probably won't let me, but I have to go and do something because if I don't, I will be up all night and by the time I get to talk to Noah, it will probably be too late."

My parents look at each other and converse without speaking.

"You can go as long as you wear the reflective vest," my mom says.

"Mom."

"We're not having you walk outside in the middle of the night without wearing the vest. End of discussion. You decide."

I go to our front closet and pull out the hideous orange polyurethane beast. I put it on and head back to my parents' room.

"Satisfied?" I ask.

"Be back by midnight."

I don't even have time to think about the words I'm going to say. I have to hope they'll be there when I need them.

Boy Loses Boy

I throw pebbles at Noah's window. Finally the light goes on. He opens the window and looks out. Then he starts throwing the pebbles back at me.

"Go away," he whisper-shouts.

"I need to talk to you," I whisper-shout back.

"But I don't need to talk to *you*."

"Please."

He closes the window and puts out the light. I linger for a minute, then give up. It was stupid to come here, stupid to expect to be treated better than I rightfully deserve.

As I hit the street, I hear a door open. Noah comes out of the house in his bare feet, and I step back onto the curb. The neighborhood is lamplight quiet. I can hear Noah take in a breath, waiting for me to speak. I look at his feet on the gravel, then at his pajama bottoms and tattered RISD T-shirt.

"Why are you wearing that stupid vest?" he asks.

"My parents made me wear it," I explain. I begin to pull it off.

"I don't remember saying you could take off your clothes," Noah says dryly. I keep the vest on.

The tone feels almost familiar. Then I remember why I am here in the dead of night.

"I'm sorry," I say, finally looking him in the eye. "I don't know what you heard or how you heard it, but I want you to know that it was something that just happened. He needed me in a really serious way, so I kissed him. Just once. Just for a moment. I wasn't thinking about you, or even about me. I was thinking about him."

I pause, then continue. "I know that doesn't make it right. And I know I'm probably not your favorite person right now. But the bottom line is that I still like you and want to be with you. I don't want to have to wait for Thursday or next week or next year. I want to talk to you and be random with you and be ridiculous with you. I don't know what I want from you, and I don't know what you want from me. If anything. What I do know, though, is that I don't want you to hate me because of one spur-of-the-moment kiss."

I stop here for his reaction. His face shows more hurt than anger. I don't know if he's going to simply walk away, or lash out at me.

"So you *did* kiss him?" he asks.

"Yeah."

"When?"

"This morning."

"This morning?"

"Yeah."

"Okay," he says. "What I want to know is this. All along, I assumed you and Tony were just friends. So does this mean it's more than that?"

I double-take.

"What do you mean?" I ask.

"I mean, is this the first time you've kissed Tony?"

"Tony?" I want to laugh.

"Yeah, Tony."

Now I'm smiling despite myself. "I didn't kiss Tony. Is *that* what you heard? Oh, God! I was in the park with him yesterday and gave him a hug because he was bummed out. That's all."

I figure this will clear things up. But Noah looks more confused than ever.

"So who did you kiss this morning, then?" he asks.

Gulp.

"Uh ... er ..."

"Uh? Er?"

Stupid. Stupid. Stupid.

"Kyle?" I say.

Noah's eyes widen. He's totally awake now.

"Your *ex-boyfriend* Kyle?"

I nod.

Now it's Noah who's laughing.

"Man," he says, "I really have *great* taste in guys. I think I'd rather have you kissing Tony. But Kyle—wow."

"I can explain," I interject, although I suppose I already *have* explained.

"Don't bother," Noah says. "Really. You weren't going to tell me, were you?"

"But I *did* tell you," I point out. I should at least have that in my favor.

Noah goes on. "When I was home over the weekend, I hung out with my three best girlfriends. I told them all about you. And you know what they said? They told me to watch out. Chloe, Angela, and Jen all said that I'm too easy on people. I think things are too good to be true, and it ends up that they *are* too good to be true. I liked you *so much*, Paul. You have no idea how hard that was for me. To come to this new town, to leave everything I love behind—and then suddenly to put all this hope and trust into a stranger. I did that with Pitt, and then—despite the fact that I *swore* I wouldn't do it again—I started to do it with you. Luckily, it didn't get that far. Luckily I'm finding this out now instead of two months from now."

I see where this is going. I want to stop it.

"Please don't do this," I say quietly.

He starts to back away. "I'm not doing it," he says. "You already did."

"It was just a kiss!"

Noah shakes his head. "It's never just a kiss. You know that. So just go home."

I am starting to cry. I have no control over it. I try to keep it in, just until he gets back inside and stops looking at me. Now he has the anger and I feel the hurt—hurt that is all the more painful because it's been self-inflicted. All he wanted was for me to be careful. And I was careless. So careless.

"Goodnight," I say as he ebbs away to his front porch.

"Goodnight," he says back—out of habit, out of kindness, who knows?

I walk home in the middle of the street, all alone with my thoughts and my frustration. Perhaps craziest of all, I still feel a flicker of hope. I know there isn't anything I can say or do right now to change Noah's mind about me. But soon right now will be minutes ago and days ago and weeks ago. What I feel about Noah can't be extinguished with one shut-down conversation. The fact that I feel so awful is a perverse proof of his worth and meaning to me.

I got myself into this mess. I can get myself out.

Or so I think.

Dealing with the Club Kids

My mother finds me the next morning as I'm deciding whether or not to get out of bed. I don't see why I get to stay home when I have a fever (something that will pass in time) and yet have to brave the lonesome hallways when there isn't a single person I'm looking forward to seeing (something that may or may not pass). I quickly try to formulate an excuse, but before I can even open my mouth, she says, "Don't even try it. And be sure to hang the safety vest back up in the closet before you go. Don't leave it on the floor like that."

Snagged on two counts. Not a great way to start the day.

I become neurotic about what to wear. Because suddenly every piece of clothing has something to do with someone else. Shirts that Jess helped me pick out. The pants I wore the night I first met Noah. The clothes from yesterday thrown over the back of the chair—it's amazing to believe that I kissed Kyle and was dumped by Noah all in the span of a single pair of jeans.

In the end I dig into the back of my closet and find a sweater my aunt got me for my birthday last year. It's orange and green, and brings out the orange in my eyes even though my eyes are usually green. The neck is a little too tight and the arms are a little too long. I wear it anyway.

I figure this is my new beginning . . . or my last resort.

The first person I bump into when I get to school is Rip, the bookie. I can tell he's been waiting for me. He stares for a moment at my sweater but doesn't say anything about it.

"So is that it, then?" he asks me. "You got no one, right?"

Technically, I figure this is true. I've lost Noah. I don't want Kyle. Tony was never an option.

I don't have anybody.

But . . .

I think again of Noah.

"The betting isn't over yet," I tell Rip.

"Seems pretty over to me," he says with a grin. I can see him counting the money in his head.

I surprise myself by clamping my hand down on his shoulder and thinking of a sports metaphor.

"Listen to me," I say. "You can't run a Super Bowl pool and then declare the winner midseason. As far as I'm concerned, we haven't even gotten to the playoffs yet. If you start collecting, I'm going to tell everyone that you're playing them for a fast one. They won't like that."

Rip thinks for a moment.

"I'll give you until the Dowager's Dance," he says finally. "That way, more people can place bets."

I nod and remove my hand from his shoulder.

As he skulks off, Infinite Darlene appears from behind me.

"Rip never dates anyone," she observes.

"Why?" I ask.

"He doesn't like the odds."

Infinite Darlene is staring at my sweater now.

"I know I should hate it," she says, "but I actually like it."

"Thanks, I think."

She is dressed immaculately in a vintage *Charlie's Angels* T-shirt and white pleather miniskirt. (I have no idea how she pulls it off. In fact, I have no idea how she pulls it on.)

"How's it going?" she asks me.

"I can't even begin to tell you," I say, then blurt out the whole story.

"Oh, honey," she says when I'm done with my wallowing, "it's like my grandma used to say: Just when you think life's got you in a gutter, a tornado will come along and destroy your house."

"And then you rebuild?" I ask.

"Well, she never mentioned that part, but I suppose it could happen."

I am not cheered up.

Then, to make matters worse, Infinite Darlene coos, "So, sweetheart, are you ready for the committee meeting sixth period?"

The dance committee meeting. I've totally forgotten about it. And I'm in charge.

Infinite Darlene continues. "I know that wench"—that would be Trilby Pope—"will be there. I know there was no way for you to stop her from signing up. So it's not like I hold *you* responsible. But please make sure she keeps her talking to a minimum. It gives me *such* a migraine."

"I'll be fair," I tell Infinite Darlene.

She sighs. "That's what I'm afraid of. Believe me, it does neither of us any favors."

With that, she swings and sashays away.

I don't see her again until sixth period, in the small room the library reserves for meetings like this. I am not at all prepared, but I'm ready to fake it.

There are ten people on the committee. The first I see are two best friends who join everything together; since their names are Amy and Emily, we call them the Indigo Girls, even though they're straight. Then there's Trilby Pope and Infinite Darlene, sitting at opposite ends of the room—Infinite Darlene is glaring at Trilby, and Trilby is simply gazing at the floor in response. I'm sure this drives Infinite Darlene crazy—she likes nothing better than a glaring match.

Kyle is in the back of the room looking a little lost. He's not on my list, and I have a sneaking suspicion he joined up late.

Then there are the Club Kids. From the start of kindergarten, they have been slaves to their college applications. They join any club available, perform every volunteer hour they can, and stab each other in the backs with sharpened No. 2 pencils in order to be valedictorian. (Ironically, the kid who's going to end up being our valedictorian, Dixie LaRue, is a total party girl who refuses to let the Club Kid pressure get to her.) Since the Club Kids tend to spread themselves thinner than Saran Wrap—with the personality to match—I know they'll probably show up for one or two committee meetings at most, put it on their résumé, and then move on to the Future Arms Merchants of America Club, or whatever.

The problem is, they always want to speak up before they leave. They feel that doing so many things qualifies them as experts in everything.

This is very rarely the case.

"I think we should have a seventies theme!" Club Kid A calls out as soon as I gather the group.

"Having a seventies theme is *so* nineties," I tell her. "Any other suggestions?"

"How about 'The Future'?" Club Kid B chimes in.

"Or 'The Diversity of Life'?" Club Kid C adds.

"How about we just go for 'Vagueness' as a theme, huh?" I interject. "This is a dance, folks—not a science fair."

Club Kid D, who'd been raising his hand, puts it down now. No doubt, he thought he was at the committee meeting for the science fair.

"How about *The Wizard of Oz*?" Club Kid E meekly proposes. I can tell from the glint in her eye that she's at least an acquaintance of Dorothy.

It's not a bad idea. But like many Club Kid ideas, it's not particularly grounded in originality. Last year's Dowager's Dance theme was *The Sound of Music*. And as much as I'd love to lay a yellow brick road down in the middle of the gymnasium and force the chaperones to dress like flying bellhop monkeys, I'm afraid it will only pale in comparison to last year, when most of the kids showed up in outfits made from their parents' old curtains.

I explain this to Club Kid E, who doesn't seem too deterred. I think there just might be hope for her yet. I ask what her name is, and she tells me it's Amber.

"Anybody else have an idea?" I ask.

"How about death?" Kyle says.

"Excuse me?"

"Death. As the theme."

We all pause for a second.

"That's the stupidest thing I've ever heard," Trilby Pope sneers.

"*I* love it," Infinite Darlene predictably disagrees.

"I'm not so sure . . . ," I say.

"No, think about it," Amy pipes up. "It could be really neat. In most cultures, dancing is part of the death ceremony. It makes life seem even cooler than it did before."

"You could decorate with images of death," Emily says.

"And people could dress up as their favorite dead person." Amy is pretty engaged right now.

"You could use tombstones as centerpieces," I say, warming up to the idea.

"I mean, someone has to dance with the portrait of the dead dowager, anyway," Kyle points out.

"You guys are *sick*," Club Kid B says.

"Shut up, Nelly," Amber interjects. "This could be better than last year's debake-off finals!"

I shoot her a blank look.

"One of the finalists from Petaluma wet his pants onstage because of the pressure," Amber explains. "It was fantastic."

"You guys aren't serious, are you?" Trilby trills.

"You wouldn't know serious if it gave you a makeover," Infinite Darlene shoots back.

"Well, at least I know how to apply *my* eye shadow."

Infinite Darlene jumps out of her seat, yelling, "Do you want to take this outside, Trilby?"

"Kicking your butt isn't worth risking a run in my stockings, *Daryl*."

I step in before Infinite Darlene can lunge at her.

"Enough!" I shout. "We're trying to architect a dance here, so crouch your tigers some other time. Infinite Darlene, sit down. Trilby, if you can't say something nice, then get the hell out of the room. Okay?"

They both nod.

"Now, let's talk a little more about death. . . ."

I'm starting to have a vision for this dance. For the rest of the period, we shoot out ideas and the architecture takes form. When the bell rings, most of us look satisfied. Club Kids A through D are a total loss, but Amber's sure to be a keeper. Trilby and Infinite Darlene have disagreed on every issue brought up, but their disagreement has at least given two points of view for the rest of us to choose between.

Amy and Emily stay a little late—they want to work some death poems into the DJ's mix. When they leave, it's only me and Kyle in the room. I feel a little awkward—the last time I saw him, I ran out of the building. I expect him to ask for an explanation. But instead he surprises me by saying, "You're really good at this, you know."

"It was your idea," I point out.

"I guess so." He pauses and studies his sneakers.

"How are you doing?" I ask. "I mean, with your aunt and all."

He looks back up at me. "Okay, I guess. My mom is really sad. I don't know what to say to her. Nothing is easy, you know?"

Some things are easy. But I realize he might not be experiencing them now.

"Thanks for asking," he adds, and it's entirely genuine.

I ask him a little more—about home, about the funeral that morning. I don't touch him, and he doesn't seem to need to be touched.

The second bell rings. We're both late for seventh period. We pack up our bags and leave together. As we do, we talk about life being unfair and the idea of a death-themed dance. We don't talk about the kiss or anything after. And I find myself thinking how strange it is—once upon a time, when we were going out, all I wanted was for Kyle to open up to me and tell me what he felt about us. Now I am grateful to him for letting us talk without having A Talk.

As far as I know, nobody besides Noah knows about what happened with Kyle and me. So it's not at all awkward to walk with him through the halls—as long as we don't bring the issue up, and as long as Noah is nowhere to be found. Since seventh period has already started, we have the hallways pretty much to ourselves. I walk him to his classroom. Once we get there, he thanks me.

I thank him back. I don't tell him what for.

More Than, Equal To, Less Than

I only see Noah once, at the end of school. He's about thirty feet away from me in the hallway. I can't decide whether to go up to him or leave him alone. By the time I choose to make a move, he's already gone.

This, it seems, is the new story of my life.

With Joni, it's even worse. She has our friend Laura tell me that she thinks I'm a jerk, and that if I'm going to be angry about her and Chuck, I might as well stay away.

"What is this, third grade?" I ask Laura.

She sighs. "To be honest, Paul—yes, it is. I didn't want to do this in the first place. I told her to talk to you herself. But she's in a mood. I can barely talk to her anymore. And if you think it's bad with you, triple that and you can begin to see how bad it is with Ted."

"Is that supposed to cheer me up?"

"No, it's meant to clear you out."

"But you don't really think I should give up, do you?"

Laura looks me right in the eye, but still it's not a direct look. I can see all of her thoughts canceling one another out.

"I don't know what to say," she says, which I take to mean that she knows exactly what to say, but she's afraid if she says it, it'll get back to Joni and she'll be joining me on the blackout list.

It's not like Joni and I haven't fought before. But it's always been about stupid things—which soda goes best with pizza, or how early you have to get to a movie if you want to be sure to get tickets. Once we didn't talk for a week because she didn't think an outfit of mine matched, when I swore up and down that it did. (Under very specific circumstances, it *is* possible to wear white socks with dark pants.) That time and all the other times we both knew we were being silly, even as our pride got caught up in the argument. We got so into it that by the end we were both at fault, which made getting back together much easier.

This time, though, it's different. This time I know she's being silly, and I know she doesn't think she's being silly at all. I blame her for blaming me. And that kind of game is hard to kick.

I decide to get all contradictory on her. I know I'm supposed to avoid her, so I search her out. I don't want Chuck to be around, so I wait until she has gym class. When there's a few minutes before the bell, I sneak into the girls' locker room.

"What the hell are you doing here?!?"

This is Joni's reaction. The rest of the girls are nonchalant. They all know I'm gay, and that their boobs mean as much as their elbows to me.

Joni's already dressed, so I know the problem is me.

"I want to talk to you," I say.

"Didn't Laura tell you to stay away?" Joni asks. She doesn't see anything weird about this sentence.

"I'd rather hear it from you."

"Stay away."

The other girls are giving us space. One comes over to back Joni up, but she waves her away.

I can recognize her anger so well. There's the way her eyes shoot fire, and the perfect D her arm forms when her fist parks against her hip.

You don't want to do this, I want to say. Which is really me saying, *I don't want you to do this.*

I've witnessed this scene before. I've heard about it a thousand times. And now here we are, and there is no question where her tone is taking us.

"Are we breaking up?" I ask quietly. Because that's what it feels like. She's dumping me as a friend.

"We were never going out," she replies sarcastically. There's a little hurt in her voice, a little bitterness. That's what I latch on to. That's what I'll take with me.

A locker door slams. Then another. Bags are slung onto shoulders. Towels are folded away. The girls around us begin to exit. I try to hold on to Joni's glance for as long as I can, hoping there will be another word to take all the other sentences back. She looks at me for a beat . . . and then she turns away. She starts putting things in her locker. She closes it. She puts on the lock (I know the combination). She is pretending I am no longer here. I had expected her to rage. I had expected her to be snide. But I hadn't expected her to make me invisible. She knows that's the thing that hurts me the most. So from her, it destroys me. I don't say another word. I want to cry in both senses of the word—I want tears, and I want to shout out. I push my way out of the locker room, out to a silent corridor between the gym and the nurse's office. I find a fire extinguisher and stare at the glass that covers it. I stare into my own washed-out face, into my own reflection. I want to break it, but I don't dare.

We were never going out. I wonder if things would have been different if I could've gone out with her, if we had been a couple at some point in our lives. We always said we had the best deal of all—friendship without sexual tension. We thought it was so uncomplicated.

"I hate the phrase 'more than friends,' " Joni told me one night not long ago. We were bundled on her couch, flipping to strange channels. "It's such nonsense. When I'm going out with someone, we're not 'more than friends'—most of the time, we're not even friends. 'More than friends' makes no sense. Look at us. There's nothing more than us."

I snuggled in close to her and vowed to never use the phrase again. But now it comes back to me, and I wonder if she's used it with Chuck, told him that they're more than friends, more than Joni and me. The only thing I can't give Joni is sex. The only thing Chuck *can* give her is sex, from what I can tell. I never thought it would be a contest between the two. And I never, ever thought that it would be a contest I would lose.

I miss Joni. I miss Noah. I don't really miss Kyle, but he's the one who finds me. Not right then, not in the halls. But later, after seventh period.

"I heard what happened," he says.

"How did you hear?" I ask.

He looks at me like I'm a freak. "You had a scene in the girls' locker room. You didn't think word would travel from there? You might as well have broken up over the PA system."

"Well, I wasn't planning on us breaking up. I was planning on us being okay."

Kyle spins a little on that one. It's like he knows he should be consoling but is unfamiliar with the language of consolation. I appreciate the mental attempt on his part, and at the same time I am relieved that he doesn't take it any further. I don't know how I'd take kindness right now. Because of Joni, I feel deserving. Because of Noah, I don't feel deserving at all.

There's something else Kyle wants to say, I can tell. But he holds that back, too.

"I was thinking we could go to the cemetery," he tells me. "All of us. For the dance. To get ideas."

"Now?"

"Um . . . tomorrow?"

I'm in no mood to argue. And I figure if our dance is going to have a death theme, there are few better places to go for inspiration than a cemetery.

Kyle goes to spread the word of our deliberately morbid field trip. I try to focus on class for the rest of the day, which is a new experience for me. In history, I try to rearrange the words on the board into a poem.

no treaty but trenches
all quiet
years to years
home in no man's land

This helps pass the time, but it doesn't do my spirits much good.

After school, I turn a corner and find Infinite Darlene talking to Noah. I can't even hide my surprise—I nearly drop my books as I pull back for a hidden view. Neither of them sees me. They talk for no more than a minute. Infinite Darlene puts her hand on Noah's shoulder and smiles. He smiles back, looking a little confused. His hair is messier than usual, his shirt half tucked. I wish for the thousandth time that I could take back all the emptiness I've given him.

As soon as he's out of the picture, I leap toward Infinite Darlene.

"Have you been spying, honey?" she asks. "You know, good girls don't spy."

"What was *that* about?"

"What was *what* about?"

"Why were you talking to Noah?"

"Darlin', it's a free country."

Now, "it's a free country" has to be the lamest reason ever invented. It's something people say when they have no other good excuse for what they've done. Hearing it come from Infinite Darlene doesn't inspire confidence.

"What are you up to?" I ask, somewhat severely.

"Don't use that tone with me," Infinite Darlene snaps. I've pushed her too far. "You're going to have to trust me on this one, okay?"

God, I wish I could trust her.

Seeing that I won't argue any further, her face brightens. "I heard what you said to Joni today. Thank you for trying."

"I wasn't trying for you. I was trying for me."

"I know. But we're all in this together. Against Chuck."

Now it's my turn to snap. "Don't you see? We're not going to win that fight. We can't be against Chuck. Being against Chuck is like being against Joni right now."

"That's how she sees it. But that doesn't mean that's how it is."

"How she sees it is *exactly* how it is. She's the one calling the shots."

"You're upset."

"Duh! Of course I'm upset."

"So you're taking it out on me."

"I am NOT TAKING IT OUT ON YOU. Sometimes it's actually not about you."

"Well, to me it is."

"Aaaaaagggggggh!" I don't want to fight with Infinite Darlene. She knows I don't want to fight with her. So I just throw my hands up in the air, scream my frustration, then move on. I can hear her laughing—*supportively* laughing—as I leave.

I want to laugh, too.

It hurts me that I can't.

To Bring You My Love

I'm walking through town on my way home from school, the sun on its way to down, the streets decorated with mailbox shadows and just-fallen leaves. I have nowhere to go (but home, eventually) and no one to see. My backpack is heavy, my thoughts even heavier. So I focus on the shops and the sky, expose my face to the wind.

I stop at the tune store, where I'm greeted by Javier and Jules. Half the store is Javier's, half is Jules's—they have entirely different musical tastes, so you have to know going in whether the tune you're looking for is more like Javier or Jules. They have been together for more than twenty years, and today as they offer me cider and argue the blues, I want to ask them how they've done it. To be together with someone for twenty years seems like an eternity to me. I can't seem to manage twenty days. Twenty weeks would be a stretch. How can they stand there behind the counter, spinning songs for each other day in and day out? How can they find things to say—how can they avoid saying things they'll always regret? *How do you stay together?* I want to ask them, the same way I want to ask my happy parents, the same way I want to go up to old people and ask them, *What is it like to live so long?*

Ella Fitzgerald croons through the speakers, then PJ Harvey lets out a forlorn cry. I flip through Javier's sale bin and see he's sneaked

134

some of Jules's tunes in there, too. Javier jokingly tells me to be careful what I wish for. Jules warns me against having too many PJ Harvey dreams.

It's colder outside when I leave, or maybe that's only because I felt so warm inside. I stop in the coffee shop to get my mother some grounds. I look to the funky puff-couches in the corner and see Cody (my first elementary school boyfriend) hanging with his new boyfriend, whose name is either Lou or Reed. They have sunk into the cushions, sharing a single cup of latte, sip by sip. Happiness rises from them like steam. Cody sees me and waves me over. I smile and gesture that I can't. I pretend I'm running out of time.

Their companionship makes me think of Noah. It makes me think about how I'd never felt that close to someone before, in that exact way.

I slip into the five-and-dime, where things still cost a nickel or ten cents. I pick up some chocolate clusters for my brother and a strand of strawberry shoestring licorice for Tony. The root beer barrels are Joni's favorite. I have to stop myself from buying those.

Next stop: the thirdhand duds store down the block. I'm searching for combat boots when I see a woman who looks almost identical to Noah. I don't want combat boots for combat; I want them because I think they'll make me feel grounded. The woman is looking at a set of slightly chipped flower pots, asking if they'll fit geraniums. Her hair is longer than Noah's, well-mannered. But the eyes are almost the same.

Suddenly Claudia comes up to her side. That's when I figure it out—I am seeing Noah's mom for the first time.

"Why don't you go look for jeans?" she suggests.

I am in the middle of the aisle. It's too late for me to move. Claudia looks right at me. If I turn around and flee, it would be the ultimate cowardice. So instead I say hi.

She walks right past me.

I figure that's her right. I find a pair of combat boots, majorly scuffed, on the bottom shelf. I fit them on and lean over to tie the laces. I hear her come back towards me. This time, she stops. With one eye on her mom, she keeps her voice low.

"If I were bigger," she says, "I swear I'd beat the crap out of you."

Then she leaves. I don't have a chance to say a word. If I did, the word would be *sorry*.

I head out without the boots—they don't fit right. Or maybe it's my mood that doesn't fit. I'm pushing the outskirts of downtown now, moving past the shops to the insurance salesfolk and the dentists' offices. I put on my headphones but can't figure whether I want a soundtrack that will reinforce my mood or combat it. I switch on the radio and decide to leave it to fate. As a result, I get five minutes of car ads.

Warnock Chevrolet's Never-ending November Sale . . . It would be a ten-minute walk to Noah's house. . . . *3.5 percent APR financing . . .* but what else could I tell him besides "sorry"? I don't have any new excuses. . . . *Act now! This offer is good for a limited time only. . . .* How could I possibly explain that he's the one my heart was made for? That's how it feels—he's the one my heart was made for.

I walk. I am dizzied by all the words I can't say to him. I sprint. I scream at myself for all that has happened. The streetlights blink on in the last remnants of sunlight. I run. I push myself harder. Harder. I want my body to be as exhausted as my heart. I want to push it farther. I want to break through. The wind pulls against me. The darkness erases all the shadows. I feel pain in my legs, a rip in my lungs. I stumble over the curb. I slow down. I gasp.

I am home.

A Very Late Night Conversation with Ted

"Gay Boy?"

"Yeah."

"It's Ted."

"Hey."

"I hope it's not too late."

"No." [pause to throw off the covers, turn on the bedside light] "Something on your mind?"

"It's Joni."

"I kind of figured." [there is no other reason he'd call me]

"Yeah."

"Yeah." [this is how guys talk]

"I can't get her off my mind."

"I hear you."

"I heard what you did today. How she wrecked you."

"It wasn't pretty."

"That's not like her. I mean, it's definitely like her to wreck people. But it's not like her to wreck *you*."

"I know."

"I mean, she's crossed a line."

"I think she knows that."

"Does she?"

"Yeah."

"You really think?"

"I think."

[long pause for thought] "I keep trying to think of something we can do. I keep wondering what it was that I did, and at the same time I know I didn't do anything. She did it this time. And she keeps doing it."

"Maybe she's just changing."

"Because of Chuck?"

"It's been known to happen."

"But not to Joni."

[noticing something in Ted's voice] "Ted?"

"Yeah?"

"Are you drunk?"

"Me?"

"Yeah."

"Not really."

"Not really?"

"Well, a little. I was just feeling so gloomy. It's never been like this before, man. It's never been this . . ."

"Difficult?"

"Hard. It's never been this hard. I know this is going to sound totally whacked, but before when we broke up, I was kind of okay with it, because I realized that she was better off without me. And maybe I was better off without her. But this time I don't feel like she's better off at all. She's dissing her friends. She's losing herself in Chuck. And she and I—well, we've lost it."

"Lost what?"

[impatient] "You know—that spark. That electricity. Even when we were broken up, we had it. She could rile me up with a simple look, and I could do the same to her. Now that's not there. And I feel—I don't know."

"You feel naked without it?"

"Naked? Hah!"

"I mean, you feel empty."

"Kind of. Is missing something proof of how much you were into it in the first place?"

[thinking again of Noah's smile] "Could be."

"So what do you do with that, Paul? What do you do with that missingness?"

"In some circumstances, you just let it go."

"Is this one of those circumstances?"

"What do you think?"

"I think no."

"I think you're right."

"So what are we going to do?"

"We're going to wait for Joni to feel the missingness, too."

"And what if she doesn't?"

[pause] "Then maybe we'll have to let it go."

[a little alarmed] "But not yet, right?"

"No, not yet."

"Because Joni's worth that, right?"

"Yeah, she is."

[hesitation] "I'm not really that drunk, okay?"

"It's okay, Ted."

"But you'll remind me of all this in the morning?"

"Yes, Ted."

"You're not that bad, Gay Boy."

"You're not too bad yourself, for a guy."

"Thanks."

"Anytime."

"But you'd prefer earlier?"

"Yeah, two's a little late."

"Cool. And hey—"

"Yeah?"

"Goodnight."

Meet Me at the Cemetery Gates

Because Amy and Emily have lacrosse practice and Infinite Darlene is prepping for the weekend's football game, we don't meet at the cemetery until the sun is going down. There is only one cemetery in our town, where people of all religions and beliefs rest side by side. Just like a community.

Although my father's parents were born and buried in another part of the country, all of my mother's family is buried here. I suppose one day my parents will be buried here, too. And even me. It's strange to walk around and think that.

In our cemetery, each tombstone has a locked box attached to it. And inside each locked box there's a book. I don't know who started this idea, or how long it's been around. But if you go to the cemetery gates, the keeper will give you the key to any box you'd like. Inside each book you will find the pages from a life. Some of the books have the dead person's own writing. Others have writing from after the death; people who come to visit the graves will write down memories and stories. Sometimes they'll write directly to the person, asking questions or giving updates on how everything turned out in the afterwards. Every now and then I'll look at my grandmother's book, which is filled with recipes and home truths. Or I'll take out a pen and add a line or two in my grandfather's book, telling him who won the World Series, if my mother hasn't already come by to fill him in.

With the keeper's permission, we are going to take some words from the memory books to include in our dance. Amy and Emily are also going to make rubbings of some of the tombstones to help decorate the walls.

As soon as Kyle arrives at the cemetery, he goes looking for something. He doesn't tell any of us what it is. He disappears.

Of all the Club Kids, Amber is the only one who shows up. She arrives with Infinite Darlene, but it's Trilby who asks her for help.

"I need to get some ideas for a dress," Trilby says. "I need some input."

Amber lets out a starstruck "Sure."

Infinite Darlene is miffed. "It won't be as good as last year's dress," she bitches.

"Oh, please," Trilby snorts. "You wanted me to wear yellow so you could take home all the boys."

"The theme was *Sound of Music*—and they were yellow *curtains*."

"Yes, but there are good curtains and there are bad curtains. You had me wearing some pretty bad curtains."

"You didn't think so at the time."

"Oh, but I'm wiser now."

To my surprise, it's Amber who steps in this time.

"Do you guys always do this?" she asks.

"Yes," Trilby and Infinite Darlene reply together. Then they try to jinx each other, but that too is simultaneous.

"And what do you get out of it?" Amber asks.

"Excuse me?" Trilby looks a little down her nose at Amber. Amber seems to fade into her overalls, but she's gone too far now to turn back.

"It's clear to everyone how much you're getting off on getting even," she observes. "Can't you just admit that?"

"No way."

"You're out of your mind."

"Am I?"

Trilby gives Amber a serious once-over. "I think I'll go look for dress ideas myself. I don't know why I asked a girl wearing OshKosh to help me in the first place."

"They're not OshKosh. They're Old Navy."

"That's not my point."

"Yeah, but it's mine."

Trilby storms off dramatically. Infinite Darlene storms off with equal drama in the opposite direction.

Amber laughs.

"Well done," I say. "I swear, if you weren't an Old Navy—wearing lesbian Club Kid, I'd probably kiss you right now."

Amber's laugh stops. She looks around to see if anyone's heard.

I've gone too far, I think.

"I'm sorry," I say.

Amber waves me off. "It's okay. It's just that I'm not ... well, I don't like to think of myself as ... a Club Kid."

She smiles again.

"I'll never think of you that way again," I promise.

"I mean, I love joining clubs and all. I just don't want word to get out, okay?"

Her secret is safe with me.

Away from the Club Kids, she's so much more sure of herself. Or maybe she's just as sure of herself when she's with the other Club Kids, only she doesn't have a chance to show it.

"Trilby and Infinite Darlene are like Nelly Peterson and George Bly," Amber observes. "Nelly and George were great friends until they started competing for valedictorian. Now it's all about the grades. They want to beat each other, and at the same time they secretly want to *be* each other. So they fight."

"And how will it end?"

"They'll either kill each other or sleep together. The jury's still out."

"But Trilby and Infinite Darlene don't want to sleep together—they want to sleep with the same people."

"Different kind of tension, same emotional results. Plus, who says they don't want to sleep together?"

"Are you saying that Infinite Darlene is a *lesbian*?"

"Stranger things have happened. And that's just in this town." Amber looks across the cemetery. "You know who I like the most in here?"

"Who?"

"The witch in the corner. She lived here two hundred years ago. Her memory book is full of spells that have been written in over the years."

"You like that?"

Amber nods. "I once went out with a witch. It didn't end well."

"What happened?"

"I didn't get along with her cat."

We are quiet again in the near dark. I realize I should be doing some serious architecting at this point, but I'm not sure what to do. Suddenly, Amy and Emily are lit by a flash as they trace gravestone inscriptions. Then another flash. Someone is taking pictures.

Noah.

Infinite Darlene sidles up behind me.

"I asked him to come," she whispered. "I figured we could use some black-and-white shots."

"You're interfering!" I accuse.

She bats an eyelash. "Of course I am. That's what friends are for."

Noah doesn't seem to notice me. He focuses on the gnarled branches reaching out to cover the emerging moon. He focuses on the angel statuary, making their wings turn a ghostly pale in one illuminated moment.

"Go over and say hello," Infinite Darlene insists.

"You're the one who invited him," I grumble.

"Yes, but you're the *host*."

I'm ready to dig in my heels and resist Infinite Darlene's meddling. Then Amber asks me, "What do you really want to do?" And I think about it. What I *want* to do is run away into the darkness. What I *really want* to do is talk to him.

So I walk over.

He is sitting on the ground now, getting a level shot of a tombstone.

"Hey," I say.

Snap and flash. My eyes take a second to readjust. He stands in the afterglow.

"Hey," he says.

It's too dark for me to see his full expression.

"I'm glad you're taking pictures," I go on. "I mean, it was a good idea."

"Did you ask Infinite Darlene to ask me?" His voice is casual curiosity, nothing more.

"No. But I should have."

"Why?"

"Because you're a really good photographer."

He thanks me and we teeter there for a moment. We are not moving, but we're teetering at the same time.

"Look . . ." *I've missed you.* Do I really have to say it? Can't he see it on my face? I'm about to say it—then I hear someone calling my name.

"Paul! You've got to come see this, Paul!"

It's Kyle. He runs over to me, not seeing Noah.

"Oh, sorry," he says when he realizes I'm not alone.

"No problem," Noah replies, raising his camera from his side.

Don't go, I want to say. But I can't say it in front of Kyle, who looks so excited to have found me.

The moment's over. Noah nods at me and Kyle, then walks away. I call out another thanks to him, but he only sends back another nod.

"Sorry," Kyle says again. "I didn't know you were—"

"He was just taking some shots of the cemetery for the dance. Infinite Darlene asked him."

We stand there for a moment, Kyle looking at me.

"You wanted to show me something?" I prompt.

"Yeah. This way."

He takes me to the dowager's crypt. I had forgotten all about it.

Kyle has lit the inside with candles, so as we approach, it looks like an elfin mansion with a fire in the grate. The outside is plain ("I won't be seeing it from the outside," the dowager is rumored to have said), but the inside is colored fifty-two different shades of blue. Every year or two they touch it up, importing paint from as far away as Cyprus to make the blue complete.

Kyle got the key to her memory book from the keeper and has been jotting excerpts into his biology notebook. I lean over to see, but he quickly closes the cover and shuffles the notebook away in his bag. I look around at the candles he's lit. They, too, are all blue.

"I wish we could have the dance in here," Kyle says, nodding to a portrait of the dowager that hangs over her tomb. It is nearly identical to the portrait that is partnered at the dance. "I think she would have liked that."

Next to the portrait is a piece of sketch paper. Kyle must have been trying to duplicate it. I walk forward for a closer look.

"I'm sorry again about interrupting," Kyle says from somewhere behind me.

"Don't worry about it," I reply, my eyes not leaving the drawing. He's changed the perspective—it's now a portrait looking slightly

145

down. The candlelight makes her expression waver, her lines blur. The thing that strikes me the most is the portrait's silence.

I feel a hand on my back. When I don't move, Kyle turns me gently around. Then he leans in and kisses me. Softly, at first. Then embracing.

My instinct kicks in, and it isn't the instinct I'm necessarily expecting. After the surprise wears off, I quietly step away. I let go of the kiss, and he lets go of my body.

"What?" he asks soothingly. "It's okay."

"No," I whisper back. "It's not."

"But it is." He takes my hand in his. I used to love it when he did that, just casually holding my hand as we had a conversation. I don't pull it away now. "I know I messed up last time," he says, "but that won't happen again. I know you're scared. I'm scared, too. But this is what I want. This is how it should be. I love you."

"Oh no!" I say. Out loud. I don't mean to. It just comes out.

Kyle laughs, but I can see his scaredness grow.

I squeeze his hand lightly. "Seriously, though. I just—" I can't find the right words.

"You just what?"

"I just don't want to. Not like that. I love you, too, but as a friend. A good friend."

He lets go of my hand. "Don't say that," he insists.

"What? I mean it, Kyle. You know I'm not just saying 'let's be friends.' "

"But you are, Paul. You are."

There's shock in his eyes now. I actually have to reach out for him because he's about to back into a candle and set his shirt on fire.

"Thanks," he says. His voice has lost all certainty. "But why did you kiss me? I thought that meant something."

I can't tell him it meant nothing. But I can't tell him it meant what he wanted it to.

"Do you regret it?" he asks, after I haven't responded.

"No," I say, even though I do.

"But you don't want to do it again?"

"I don't think we should."

"And you know what you want."

I nod.

"You always know what you want, don't you?"

"That's not true," I say, thinking about the last two weeks. "And that's not fair."

"No," Kyle agrees. "It's not fair at all." He is back by his book bag now, gathering his things. "I thought this would work. I thought it would be a perfect way to start again. But I forgot about you. I forgot how easy it is for you."

"Easy?"

"Yes," Kyle says, punctuating the phrase by throwing down his things. "*Easy*. Paul, you don't know how lucky you are."

"How am I lucky?"

"Because *you know who you are*. Most of the time, Paul, I have no idea what I want. And then when I do, something like this happens. You make me feel so low, when all I want is to be with you."

I could point out that he used to make me feel the same way, but I've already forgiven him for that. I could point out that it isn't always easy knowing who you are and what you want, because then you have no excuse for not trying to get it. I could point out that right now—*even now*—I am still thinking about the few words I just exchanged with Noah. I could point out any number of things. But I am entirely disarmed, because now Kyle is shivering in front of me, holding in his tears as he picks up his bag. "I'm sorry," I say, but I know this isn't enough. There isn't a single phrase for all the things I need to say—there isn't a single sentence that will explain how I want to hug Kyle into security but don't want to kiss him. He is walking around the crypt now, not looking at me, not saying another word. He blows out the candles one by one. I stand where I am and say his name. The last candle is on top of the dowager's tomb. Kyle leans over and extinguishes it. We are left in a darkness of blues. I say his name again. But the only response comes from the sound of his leaving.

Tony

I ask Amber to call Tony's house for me. When he answers, she passes the phone my way and I ask if I can come over. He says there's about an hour before his mother will be back from her prayer circle.

Emily gives me a ride. From her respectful silence, I can tell that she's pieced together Kyle's departure, my agitation, my own departure, and my need for respectful silence. She's probably figured out a close variation of the real story.

Tony's front door is unlocked. I head right to his room. After one look at my face, he asks me what happened, and I tell him.

As I talk, clocks chime throughout the house. A floorboard creaks under ghost steps. Alert, we listen for the sound of the garage door opening or a key turning in the back door.

I tell Tony about Noah. I tell Tony about Kyle and all the things he said. I show him my confusion, my hurt, my anger—I don't hold anything back. As usual, Tony reserves his words until the end, prompting me with nods and listening.

I expect him to tell me that Kyle is off base, that he'd been speaking out of confusion, hurt, and (yes) anger, not truth. But instead Tony says, "Kyle's right, you know."

"What?" I heard him the first time, but I want to give him the option to change his mind.

"I said, Kyle's right. I know exactly where he's coming from."

I'm so taken aback by what Tony's saying that I look away from him. I look at all the chaste decorations in his room, all the child-hood relics—baseball cards, sports car ads—that he hasn't been able to replace with the telltale signs of his present life. Everything that's visible in this room is exactly the same as when I first saw it. Only the hidden parts have changed.

"Paul," Tony continues, "do you know how lucky you are?"

Of course I know this. Although I have to admit I always tend to think of other people as unlucky rather than thinking of my own life as charmed.

"I know I'm lucky," I say, perhaps a little defensively. "But that doesn't mean it's easy. Kyle said it's easy for me."

"That's not a bad thing, Paul."

"Well, the way he said it, it was. And the way you're saying it, too."

Tony is sitting cross-legged on the floor, playing with a thread from his sweater.

"The first time I met you," he says, not directly to me, not directly to the floor—somewhere in between, "I honestly couldn't believe that someone like you could exist, or even a town like yours could entirely exist. I thought I understood things. I thought I would get up every morning with a secret and go to sleep every night with the same secret. I thought my life would start only when I was out of here. I felt that I had learned something about myself too soon, and that there was nothing I could do to undo the truth. And I wanted to undo it, Paul. I wanted to so bad. Then I met you in the city and on the train, and suddenly it was like this door had been opened. I saw I couldn't live like I'd been living, because now there was another way to do it. And part of me loved that. And part of me still hates it. Part of me—this dark, scared part of me—wishes I never knew how it could be. I don't have the courage that you do."

"That's not true," I say quietly. "You are so much braver than I am. You face all these things—your parents, your life."

"Kyle feels lost, Paul. That's all he's saying. And he knows that you're not lost. You've never really been lost. You've *felt* lost. But you've never *been* lost."

"And are you lost? Do you feel lost?"

Tony shakes his head. "No. I know exactly where I am, what I'm up against. I'm on the other side, Paul."

I can hear all the emptiness in the house. I can see the way the pennants droop away from the walls of his room. I know that he's not happy, and it breaks my heart.

"Tony," I say.

He shakes his head again. "But this isn't about me, is it? It's about you and Noah and Kyle and what you're going to do."

"I don't care about any of that," I tell him. "I mean, I care about it. But not right here, right now. Talk to me, Tony."

"I didn't want to bring this up. Forget I said anything."

"No, Tony. Tell me."

"I don't know if you want to hear it."

"Of course I want to hear it."

"I love being with you and Joni and the rest of the group. I love being a part of that. But I can never really enjoy it, because I know that at the end, I'll be back here. Sometimes I can forget, and when I can forget, it's bliss. But this past week has been hell. It's like I've been pushed back into the shape of this person I used to be. And I don't fit into the old shape anymore. I don't fit."

"So leave," I say—and the minute I say it, I'm full of the idea. "I'm serious. Let's pack up your things. You can live at my house. I'm sure my parents will take you in. Then we can figure things out. We can find you a room somewhere—maybe in that room over Mrs.

Reilly's garage. You don't have to be here, Tony. You don't have to live like this."

I'm getting all excited. It's like an airlift. Tony is a refugee. We need to get him to a better place.

It seems so simple to me. But Tony says, "No, I can't."

"What do you mean?"

"I can't, Paul. I can't just leave. I know you won't understand this, but they love me. It would be much easier if they didn't. But in their own way, they love me. They honestly believe that if I don't straighten out, I will lose my soul. It's not just that they don't want me kissing other guys—they think if I do it, I will be damned. *Damned*, Paul. And I know that doesn't mean anything to you. It really doesn't mean anything to me. To them, though, it's everything."

"But they're wrong."

"I know. But they don't hate me, Paul. They honestly love me."

"Part of love is letting a person be who they want to be."

Tony nods. "I know."

"And they're not doing that."

"But maybe they will someday. I don't know. All I know is that I can't just run off. They think that being gay is going to mess up my whole life. I can't prove them right, Paul. I have to prove them wrong. And I know I can't prove them wrong by changing myself or by denying what I really am. The only way for me to prove them wrong is to try to be who I am and show them it's not hurting me to be that way. In two years I'll graduate. I'll be gone. But in the meantime, I have to find a way to make this work."

I am so scared for him. I realize that what he's saying is beyond my scope of comprehension. What he wants to do is more than I've ever had to do.

"Tony," I say, "you're not alone in this."

He leans back against his bed. "Sometimes I know I'm not, and sometimes I really think I am. I don't like to get into the middle of things, but sometimes I stay awake at night, petrified that we're all scattering apart. And I know I'm not strong enough to keep us all together and keep myself together at the same time. Plus, you're in love, Paul. You might not call it that, but that's what it is. And I don't want to be the downer to your upper. I know there are only so many things you can float at once."

I don't let him finish the thought. "I'm here," I tell him. "I will always be here. And I know I've been overwhelmed by the past week. And I know you can't always count on me to do the right thing. But I want to help."

"I don't know if I can do it, Paul." I can tell he wants to. He's decided he wants to.

"You have a much better chance than I would," I say. "You are so much braver than me."

"That's not true."

"Yes it is."

The garage door opens. Both Tony and I tense up.

"I'll go," I say, gathering my things, planning a quick escape.

Tony looks up at me and says, "No, don't."

The garage door is closing now.

"Are you sure?" I ask. I don't know what kind of trouble this will bring. All I know is that whatever he wants me to do, I'll do it.

"I'm sure."

The door to the basement. Tony's mother calling his name.

"I'm in here with Paul!" he yells.

Silence. Keys on the front counter. A pause. Footsteps on the stairs.

All those years of us pretending. All the "bible study groups" and midnight curfews. All those times we had to wash the scent of a basement rave out of Tony's clothes, or let Tony onto our computers to go places his parents wouldn't let him go. All those moments of panic when we thought we wouldn't make it back on time, when we thought that Tony would come home and the door would be locked for good. All those lies. All those fears. And now Tony's mother coming into the room—not even knocking—and seeing the two of us sitting on his floor, him cross-legged and leaning on the side of his bed, me kneeling by the bookcase, not even pretending to be looking for a book.

"Oh," she says—the kind of word that falls like a stone.

"We're going to do some homework," Tony says.

She looks straight at him. "I'm not sure that's a good idea."

All those silences. All those burning thoughts kept hidden. And now Tony is letting them out, carefully. Now Tony is standing his ground.

"Why?" Tony asks—the kind of word that is thrown like a stone.

"Why?" Tony's mom repeats—an off-guard echo, an uncertain response.

"Paul is my best friend, and we've been doing homework together for a long time. He is my *friend*—nothing more, no different from Joni or Laura or any other girl. I am being totally honest with you, and I want you to be totally honest with me. Why could you possibly think it's a bad idea for Paul and me to do our homework together?"

I see it in her eyes. I see exactly what Tony was talking about. That strange, twisted, torn love. That conflict between what your heart knows is right and what your mind is told is right.

He's called her on it. And she doesn't know how to respond.

"I don't want to talk about this right now," she says. Her body language is pretending I'm not in the room.

"We don't have to talk about it. But Paul's going to stay until he has to go home for dinner."

"Tony, I'm not sure about that."

"We'll leave the door open. We can even go into the kitchen if you want us to. There are some girls at school whose parents have those rules when boys come over, even if they're just friends, so I guess that would make sense for me, too."

If I told this to my parents, there'd be an element of challenge in it, or sarcasm. But Tony's speaking is plain and simple. He is not crossing the line into snarkiness. He is making his point, but being perfectly respectful in tone.

I wish I could know what thoughts are going through his mom's mind right now. Is she trying to dismiss this away? *Oh, it's just a phase* or *It must be that evil Paul's influence—he's the one to blame.* Is she devastated that Tony is beyond "saving"? Is she cursing fate—or even God—for putting her in this situation? Is she embracing it as a challenge? I can see her thinking, but I don't know the thoughts. I am sitting no more than five feet away from her, but she's in a different world.

She looks at the walls, inhales and exhales.

"Leave the door open," she says. "I'll be in the kitchen."

Tony is speechless. He merely nods. His mom doesn't nod in return. She backs away, out of the door, down the steps. Tony looks at me. I burst out smiling. I clap without making a sound. He smiles, too. Then his smile falls and all of a sudden he is sobbing. He is shuddering and shaking and gasping. He has kept all this white noise inside him, and now some of it is coming out. His face is newborn raw, his arms wrap around his body. I move over to him and hug him tight. I tell him that he's brave. I tell him that he's done it—he's taken not the first step (that happened a long time ago) but the next step. His cry carries through the house. I rock him a little and look up to see his mother in the doorway again. This time I can read her perfectly. She wants to be where I am, holding him. But I know she will not say the things I am willing to say. Maybe she knows this, too. Maybe this will change, too. She looks at my face and gives me a nod. Or maybe she is finally returning Tony's nod. Then she retreats again.

"I'm sorry," Tony says, sniffling back into composure.

"There's nothing to be sorry about," I tell him.

"I know."

I find my greatest strength in wanting to be strong. I find my greatest bravery in deciding to be brave. I don't know if I've ever realized this before, and I don't know if Tony's ever realized it before, but I think we both realize it now. If there's no feeling of fear, then there's no need for courage. I think Tony has been living with his fear for all his life. I think now he's converting it to courage.

Do I tell him this right now? I would, only he changes the subject. And I let him, because it's his subject to change.

"What are you going to do about Noah?" he asks.

"Why don't you ask me what I'm going to do about Kyle?" I'm curious.

"Because there's nothing you can do about Kyle right now. But you need to do something about Noah."

"I know, I know," I say. "The only problem being that (a) he thinks I'm getting back with my ex-boyfriend, (b) he thinks I'll only hurt him, because (c) I've already hurt him and (d) someone else has already hurt him, which means that my hurting him hurt even more. So (e) he doesn't trust me, and in all fairness, I (f) haven't given him much reason to trust me. Still, (g) every time I see him, I (h) want everything to be right again and (i) want to kiss him madly. This means that (j) my feelings aren't going away anytime soon, but (k) his feelings don't look likely to budge, either. So either (l) I'm out of luck, (m) I'm out of hope, or (n) there's a way to make it up to him that I'm not thinking of. I could (o) beg, (p) plead, (q) grovel, or (r) give up, but in order to do that, I would have to sacrifice my (s) pride, (t) reputation, and (u) self-respect, even though (v) I have very little of them left and (w) it probably wouldn't work anyway. As a result, I am (x) lost, (y) clue-free, and (z) wondering if you have any idea whatsoever what I should do."

"Show him," Tony tells me.

"Show him?"

"Show him how you feel."

"But I've told him. That night. I made it clear to him how I felt. My words were out there. He didn't want them."

"Don't tell him, Paul. Show him."

"And how do I do that?"

Tony shakes his head. "I'm not going to tell you. But I have a feeling that if you think hard about it, you'll figure out how to do it. If you want to be loved, be lovable. It's a good place to start."

I think about what's just happened. I think about bravery. The risk of making a fool of myself in front of Noah is nothing compared to what Tony's just done. Nothing.

The Snoopy on Tony's clock is doing a disco-Travolta pose. It's time for me to go home for dinner.

"Do you want me to stay?" I ask.

Tony shakes his head. "I'll be okay," he tries to assure me.

"But your father . . . ?"

"I'll deal with it."

"You don't have to deal with it by yourself."

"I know. But it would be better if you weren't here. My dad's actually more of a pushover than my mom, as long as things are a little out of sight." He knows what I'm about to say. "I know that's not right, Paul, but that's the way things are. And right now, I'm going to have to work with the way things are."

I nod. "Call me," I say.

"I will," Tony replies. He sounds so sure of it, I believe him.

Three hours later, he calls. My mom answers the phone.

"Tony!" she says, all happiness. "It's so good to hear your voice! I've been stocking up on macadamia nuts, so you'd better come over soon. I can even pick you up or drive you home, just like old times. You're always welcome here."

(Man, I love her.)

"In the next election, I'm voting for your mom to be the next God," Tony says when I pick up the phone.

"How did it go?"

"Well . . ." Tony's voice sounds a little glum. "I'm afraid you're not going to see the inside of my bedroom for a while."

"Tony—"

"But you *will* be able to see a lot of my kitchen. Just be sure to keep your hands to yourself, okay?"

This is what a small victory feels like: It feels like a little surprise and a lot of relief. It makes the past feel lighter and the future seem even lighter than that, if only for a moment. It feels like rightness winning. It feels like possibility.

I was the first openly gay president of my third-grade class. I have seen men holding hands walking down the street in a big city and I have read about women being married in a state that's not so far away. I have found a boy I just might love, and I have not run away. I believe that I can be anyone I might want to be. All these things give me strength. And so does something as simple as talking to Tony on the phone after curfew, hearing that we'll be hanging out in his kitchen without having to lie.

It is, as I said, a victory. It might not last, but right now it means everything to me.

Possibly Maybe

It's a fine line between love and stalking. I decide to walk it. I want to do right by Noah. Show him, Tony said. But really, I'm guided more by what Tony's shown me. I will not hesitate to say who I love.

On the first day, I give him flowers and time.

The night before, I unlock my closet of origami paper—over a thousand sheets of bright square color. I turn them all into flowers. Every single one. I do not sleep. I do not take breaks. Because I know that as well as giving him the flowers, I am giving him the time it takes to make them. With every fold, I am giving him seconds of my life. With every flower, part of a minute. I tie as many as I can to pipe-cleaner stems. I arrange bouquets and lattices, some topped by cranes. In the morning, I garland them throughout the halls, centerpiecing it all at his locker, so he'll know that they're all for him.

Every minute, every crease is a message from me.

On the second day, I give him words and definitions.

This isn't to say I talk to him—no, I don't do that at all. Instead, I start a list of the words I love—

resplendent
giddy
trollop

—and then I add definitions—

resplendent—shining brilliantly
giddy—lighthearted and flighty
trollop—an untidy or immoral woman

Soon I decide to look randomly through the dictionary to find other unique words and definitions. I do this at Tony's kitchen table, with Tony at my side. We decide this isn't homework that we can swap—it needs to come from me.

scrappage—material broken into scrap
mucronate—having an abruptly projecting point, like a leaf or a feather
frequentation—the act of frequenting

Tony's mother drops by the kitchen twelve times in the first hour. First she asks if we need anything. After a while she pretends to need something herself—scissors from the drawer, a phone number from the kitchen notepad. Does she honestly believe that I will suddenly start ravishing her son on the kitchen table if she doesn't interrupt to get a glass of water every ten minutes? I guess there's no way to assure her I won't. Instead, we confuse her with my assignment, as I read aloud all the words that I find, simply by flipping to a page and choosing a word that I like.

debauchery—indulgence in sensual pleasures
azure—sky blue
isochronal—equal or uniform in time

Tony tells me he's been thinking of calling Kyle, just to see if he's okay.

"He probably needs someone to talk to," he says, "and it can't be you."

I know it can't be me, and say so. I think it's cool that Tony could help him with things. I don't know why it has never occurred to me before, but I can really see them getting along.

prophetic—predictive, especially when ominous
vitreous—of the nature of glass
dulcet—pleasant to the ear; melodious

The words don't have anything in common. But that's what I like about them. There are so many words in our language; we get to know so few of them. I want to share some of the strangers with Noah.

After I jot down the words—a hundred in all—I rewrite them nicely on a long scroll, under the heading

Words to Find and Know in this World

I tie the scroll with a ribbon that Tony salvages from his room, a ribbon from a gift Joni gave him for his last birthday. I ask Tony if he's talked to Joni lately. He says, "Kind of," but doesn't explain.

I leave the scroll of words and definitions at Noah's locker at the beginning of the day. At the end of the day, I find a scrap of paper in my own locker. Noah has given me a word of his own invention.

literogratumerriment—thanks for the words

On the third day, I give him space.

It's Saturday, and I decide to leave him alone. I put a letter in his mailbox wishing him a good day. I don't want to overwhelm him with everything. I also want to give him (and myself) time to think.

On the fourth day, I give him a song.

Zeke has come down to the dance hall because he's going to favor us with some tunes for next weekend's dance. I explain my situation to him, and he offers me some of his troubadour vibe. He asks me how I feel about Noah, and I tell him all my thoughts — from the goofy to the sublime, the ridiculous to the tried-and-true. I give him materials of longing, materials of hope, and, like an expert quiltmaker, he sews them together into something grand and entire.

The whole dance committee (all but Kyle, who's opted out of the day) pauses to listen, then breaks out in applause when Zeke is through. Triumphant, he gathers us in his notes and leads us from the school gym into the streets, proud pied piper, swaying and grooving to his strum until we are all on Noah's doorstep, a parade of well-wished well-wishers delivering a song. Amber pushes me to the front, next to Zeke.

"But I can't sing," I whisper to him.

"I think he'll know it's not from me, even if I'm the one who sings."

We call up to the bedroom. Claudia comes to the door, shoots us all an evil glare, then says Noah is in his studio. We prevail upon her to get him. Finally he comes to his bedroom window.

Zeke's voice fills the air with sweetness.

there is a once
when I never think twice
you give me that, boy
you give me that

there is a kind
which is much more than nice
you give me that, boy
you give me that

and now it's time for me to reveal
all the parts of me you've helped become real
to feel

there is a go
that turns into a stay
you give me that, boy
you give me that

there is a dream
which goes its own way
you give me that, boy
you give me that

and still sometimes I feel so much fear
there are parts of me I want to make clear
from here

there is a true
which never rings wrong
I'll give you that, boy
I'll give you that
there is a word
in search of a song
I'll give you that, boy
I'll give you that

let me give you that
I promise
I promise
to give you that
a dream, a song
a never of wrong
a once, a twice
a much more of nice
a love, a love
a floating of love
I'll give you that, boy
I promise
I promise
to give you that

Throughout the song, Noah looks at me and looks at Zeke. When he looks at Zeke, I study him like you study a baby, waiting for its next expression. When he looks at me, I quickly look away. I cannot hold his glance, not until I know he's meaning for me to have it.

When the song is over, Noah smiles and applauds. Zeke bows slightly, then leads everyone back to the gym. I am the last one to go, watching Noah fade back behind his blinds. I walk slowly, wondering what to do next.

He catches up to me and touches my shoulder.

"You don't have to do this," he says.

I tell him I do.

"I'm showing you," I say.

"Okay," he says.

We leave it at that.

On the fifth day, I give him film.

I use money I've saved to buy twenty rolls of film, some of them black-and-white, some of them bright outdoor color. On the top of each container I write a word from a quote I'd found from an old photographer: *Whether looking to mountains or studying the shadow of a branch, it is always best to keep your vision clear.*

In order to give the film to Noah in a creative way, I need willing accomplices. Tony, Infinite Darlene, Amber, Emily, Amy, Laura, and Trilby are more than happy to help. Even my brother gets into the act, offering to be a delivery boy after I tell him my plan.

Each accomplice gives Noah the film in a unique way. Tony starts it all off by calling Noah's cell phone and leaving a riddle that leads him to the first roll, which I've left sitting atop seat 4U in the school auditorium. Infinite Darlene makes fake-fur stoles for her containers and delicately hands them over throughout the day. Amber creates a Kodak-sized slingshot and fires the rolls into Noah's bag when he's not looking (and sometimes when he is). Emily and Amy draw faces on their canisters and give them to Noah as a family unit. Laura places the film in mysterious places where she knows Noah will find it (like stuck to the bottom of his desk). Trilby paints her canister the school colors. My brother, bless his heart, simply walks up to Noah and says, "Here, my brother wanted me to give you this." Perfect.

Even Ted offers to help. He still looks a little unsteady—rumor has it that he's looking for a rebound from his rebound. I've already distributed all the film, so I promise him he's my #1 sub if anyone falls through. Neither of us mentions Joni, but she's there in our every encounter.

It still feels strange not to have Joni on my side. (It's not that she's joined someone else's side—she's just left the field entirely.) I wonder if anyone's told her what's going on. I see her in the halls, always with Chuck, never really looking at me. At this time last year, she was helping me hang signs for the Dowager's Dance, telling me when I'd taped up the posters crooked and helping me fix them. If I could get a sense from her that she missed me—or, at the very least, that she missed our past—I would feel better. But this total shutting off makes even the past seem sad and doomed.

On the sixth day, I write him letters.

I know I only have a day left. I know when he leaves me a note thanking me for the film that the time will soon come to talk to him, to see if I have a chance. But instead of confronting it right out, I decide to write him back. At first it starts as a note, telling him I'm sure he'll put the film to good use. Then it turns itself into a letter. I can't stop writing to him. I barely pay attention in any of my classes, pausing only to notice images and incidents that I can share with Noah in the letter. It isn't entirely different from when I was writing him notes in class, before everything happened. But it feels more intense. A note is an update or an entertainment. A letter is giving of a part of your life—an insight into your thoughts beyond mere observations.

I finish the first letter. I bum an envelope off my guidance counselor and seal the pages inside. Instead of relying on my friends, I deliver it to Noah myself. He seems a little surprised, but not unreceptive. I immediately start the second letter, beginning with the moment I handed him the first letter and what was going through my mind. Suddenly the whole week begins to explain itself—I am telling instead of showing, but that seems okay, since I've already tried to show so much.

I am writing my third letter to Noah in study hall when Kyle sits down across from me. Ever since the cemetery incident, he's dodged me. But now it's clear he wants to talk. I cover the letter I'm writing and say hello.

He's nervous.

"Look," he says, "I don't want it to be this way again."

"Neither do I."

"So what are we going to do?"

I realize at this moment that Kyle is brave, too. I want to be worth his courage.

"We're going to be cool with each other," I say carefully. "We're going to be friends. And I really mean that. Just because I don't think we'd be good together doesn't mean we have to be apart. Does that make sense?"

Kyle nods. "Yeah."

"So we're good?"

"The last couple of days I've been talking to Tony. But you probably know that. At first when he called, I thought, what's going on here? It was probably the first time he'd ever called me, except for the times you were over and he was calling for you. I didn't know what to say to him, and he totally understood that. We've been talking a lot now, and the funny thing is that part of me is glad that all this happened, because if I become friends with him and I'm really friends with you, then it's like the good coming out of the bad. And the bad isn't really that bad. I feel silly about the other day. I thought something was there that wasn't. But now maybe I think something's there that's actually there."

"It is," I tell him.

I can't let him know that the something he thought wasn't there wasn't *entirely* not there. I can't tell him that some of my feelings for him will always be unresolved, and that part of the desire to have him back in my life was to disprove all the reasons he left in the first place. I can't point out to him that right now I like him more than I did in the dowager's crypt—even though I'm not liking him in the way that he wanted me to (Noah has the monopoly on that), I *am* liking him enough to know that a different time and a different place might have led to a different outcome. But since I'm not planning on leaving this time or place anytime soon, it's not a point worth making.

We start talking about the dance some more. Now that the awkwardness has lifted, Kyle's going to start showing up again at our committee and help with the final architecture.

When Kyle's gone, I finish my third letter to Noah. The fourth I slip into his hand as he leaves school. The fifth is the one I take home with me, saving it for the next day.

Instinct and Proof

On the seventh day, I give him me.

I do this by going over and saying hi. I do this by dissolving the distance between us. I do this not knowing how he'll react. Perhaps this will be the one thing that I give to him that he returns.

I find him in the morning because I don't think I can wait until the afternoon. He hasn't even hit his locker yet—I wait for him on the school steps, the morning light still new. He sees me and I walk over. I hand him my fifth letter and say hello. The envelope is green. When he holds it up, it brings out the green of his eyes.

"Paul . . . ," he begins.

"Noah . . . ," I begin.

"I don't know what to say." The tone of his voice is more *I don't know what to say because I'm speechless* instead of *I don't know what to say because you're not going to like what I have to say.* This is a good sign.

"You don't need to say anything."

We sit down next to each other on the steps. Other kids walk into the school around us.

"Thanks for the letters. I re-read them all last night."

I imagine him in his wonderful room. I'm glad my words have been there, even if I've been banished.

"I wanted to write you back," he continues. "But then I decided to do something else instead."

He pulls an envelope out of his bag and hands it to me. My hands are shaking a little when I open it. Inside I find four photographs. They are snapshots from our town, flashes from the night. Each one is a single word, but I am so familiar with the town that I can tell where they come from as well as what they say.

From the sign outside the Jewish Community Center: *wish*

From a Lotto advertisement outside the stationery store: *you*

From the inscription on the cemetery gates: *were*

And then, the last photo—Noah reflected in a mirror he's placed in his studio. One hand holds the camera to his eye. The other is holding a sheet of construction paper, with a single word written on it.

Here.

I look at these images and it's like they're the only thing I've ever wanted. How could he know that?

"Serendipity," he says. "I was up all night developing. I took photos of a hundred words, and these were the ones I wanted. That's what my instinct told me."

"And what's your instinct telling you to do now?" I ask him. I feel entirely undeserving.

There's a pause.

Then he says, "It's telling me to ask you to the dance on Saturday."

I twinkle. "So what are you going to do?"

"Do you want to go with me to the dance on Saturday?"

"I'd love to. It's not that kind of dance—people don't have to ask dates or anything—but I would love to be your date anyway."

I can't leave it at that. I have to add, "I'm sorry about everything."

And he looks at me and says, "I know."

"I've missed you so much," I say, reaching up to touch his face.

He leans in and kisses me once. He says he's missed me, too.

I know this is right. I know he's not going to be amazing all the time, but there's more amazingness in him than in anyone else I've known. He makes me want to be amazing, too.

I float through the day. Of course everybody who helped me out over the past week wants to know how it ended up. All they need to do is take one look at me and they know.

"Way to go!" Amber cheers.

Ted punches me on the shoulder. It hurts, but I know he means well.

Infinite Darlene says, "Don't mess it up again, honey."

I tell her I won't.

I swear that I won't.

Even Kyle hears. He doesn't say anything to me about it, but when we pass in the hall he gives me a silent nod of approval.

After school, I meet up with Noah and we head to the I Scream Parlor. He gets a blood-red sundae while I get the sorbet with gummi worms in it. He tells me what's been going on with him (his parents were in and are now back out of town), and I tell him what's been going on with me. I tell him about the whole Joni saga, and about what Tony's been through.

"We should go over there, cheer him up," Noah suggests.

"Are you sure?" I ask. It's not like he and Tony are friends, really.

"Yeah. We have to stick together, right?"

"Absolutely."

We call my brother, who's more than happy to take us to Tony's. (He also seems happy that I'm with Noah; I didn't know Jay had it in him.)

Tony's on the phone with Kyle when we get there. Caught up in the happiness of things, I almost tell Tony to invite him over. Then I realize what a colossally awkward move that would be (with Noah there) and keep my big mouth shut.

Even though Tony's parents aren't home, we stick to the kitchen. This works well, because we're all in high snacking gear. If we'd been stranded in the dining room, we'd be in big trouble.

"I have some news," Tony tells us. I love how he's welcomed Noah as if it's natural for him to be here. I love how Noah fits right in.

"What's your news?"

"I want to go to the Dowager's Dance."

This *is* news. Last year, Tony's parents wouldn't let him go.

"Great," Noah says. "You can come with us."

Tony sighs. "It's not that easy. You see, my parents say I can't go. But I want to go anyway. I don't want to sneak out—that would be a bad scene."

"So what are you—what are *we* going to do?" I ask.

"Here's the thing. I figure if enough people come to pick me up—if my parents see it's a whole big group of girls and guys—then maybe they'll let me go."

"Sounds like a plan," I say. "We can gather everyone up."

"I'm in," Noah volunteers.

"As am I. Jay can drive us. I'm sure we can get Laura and Emily and Amy and Amber—"

"Who's Amber?" Tony asks.

I've forgotten how new Amber is to my life.

"She's this girl on the committee. You'll love her."

"Oh yeah—Kyle's told me about her."

I have to ask. "So will Kyle come, too?"

Tony nods. "He's in."

"And Joni?"

Now Tony's look wavers.

"I don't know," he says.

"Have you asked her?"

"Yeah."

"And?"

"She wants to. . . ."

"But?"

"I don't think Chuck wants to."

"I don't see what one thing has to do with the other," I say. But of course I do. I know exactly what's going on, and it makes me furious. I am so angry at Joni right now. Words can't describe it. I don't mind her dissing me. Dissing Tony is beyond excuse.

I know Tony will feel even worse if I show him how bothered I am. So I start talking about the dance itself. Noah reaches into his book bag and takes out some of the photos he took in the cemetery. They are extraordinary—spooky, but in a spiritual way. I can tell Tony's as impressed as I am. At one point when Noah has to go to the powder room (we figure this is allowed, even if it isn't in the kitchen), Tony gives me this all-knowing look and smiles.

"It's all because of you," I say. "You told me to show him and I did. Honestly, I wouldn't have trusted myself to do it if you hadn't suggested it."

"It was all you," he says back. "And was it worth it?"

I nod as Noah comes back into the room.

"What?" Noah asks, sensing he's walking into the middle of a conversation.

"Nothing," Tony and I say at once, then look at each other and laugh.

"We were just talking about you," Tony says.

"Only bad things, I assure you," I add.

Noah takes it in stride. After an hour of hanging out and homeworking, Jay returns and Noah and I take our leave. Jay drops Noah off at his house; I walk him to the door. He ruffles my hair a little before he goes inside. I ruffle him back. We smile and say good-bye. We look forward to hello.

When I get back to the car, Jay turns for home. But I tell him we have one more stop to make.

I need to talk to Joni. Now.

Flicker

Joni's mom is surprised to see me. She also seems relieved.

"Paul!" she exclaims after opening the door. "It's so good to see you."

"You too," I say — and it's true. She's like a second mom to me. One of the hardest things about losing Joni is that I've lost my second family, too.

"Is Joni home?" I ask.

"She's upstairs. A couple of weeks ago, she asked me not to let you in if you ever showed up. But you can come right in."

It's a sign of how little I know Joni anymore that I'm actually afraid of getting her mom in trouble.

"Are you sure?" I say to her.

"As sure as sure can be," she answers. "I know you two have had some sort of falling-out, and in my opinion the sooner you get past it, the better. So go right up. Chuck left about an hour ago. I think they're on the phone."

I don't ask Joni's mom what she thinks of Chuck — I know that's totally against the rules — but I sense from her voice that she's not his biggest fan. Or maybe I'm just hearing what I want to hear.

If you stripped me of my five senses, I would still be able to find my way to Joni's bedroom from the front door. The only thing that's changed since first grade is the size of my steps.

Her door is closed. I knock.

"Not now! I'm on the phone!"

I knock again. I can hear her walk across the room.

"One sec," she says into the phone. Then, "What is it, Mom?"

As she opens the door I say, "It's not your mom. It's me."

"I can see that," Joni deadpans. She doesn't put down the phone.

"I need to talk to you."

"I'm busy."

I want to hang up the phone for her. I restrain myself, and simply make it clear that I'm not going to leave.

She stares at me hard, then says "I gotta go" into the phone.

"There," she tells me as she hangs up. "Are you happy?"

Why are you doing this? I want to scream. *What did I do to you?*

I have to remind myself that this isn't about us. It's about Tony.

"I was just at Tony's," I say.

"I talked to him two days ago. Sounds like he's doing well."

I nod. "He's doing amazingly well."

"Thanks for the report."

I won't let her light my fuse. I won't be the one to blow up.

"I want to talk to you about the night of the dance. Tony wants us to pick him up. I want to make sure you can."

Joni shakes her head. "I don't think that's going to work out. Sorry."

"*Sorry?!?* That's it?"

"What else do you want, Paul?"

"Joni, this is Tony we're talking about. Do you know what hell he might have to go through in order to go to the dance?"

"I understand that. But I have other plans. I can support him in other ways. I don't need to be there."

Does she really believe this? I see a flicker of doubt in her eyes.

"Of course you need to be there," I stress. "This is the first time that Tony's ever asked us for anything, Joni. *Anything.* He's doing the one thing we've always wanted him to do—he's standing up to his parents. He wants us there. Both of us."

"If he'd come up with this idea a week ago, or even a few days ago, I might have been able to rearrange things. But we made promises, Paul. We made plans. I can't just back out."

"Why—won't Chuck let you?"

Joni straightens to full height. "Don't go there, Paul," she warns in an icy voice.

"Why not, Joni? After all, I'm not going to tell you anything you don't already know."

There. I am the one who crosses the line. I hope she's happy.

Now I have to leave before she tells me to get out. I need that, at least.

"You know the right thing to do," I say. Then I turn and leave. I don't slam the door. I don't stomp down the stairs. I don't forget to say good-bye to her mom, who gives me a true hug.

I walk home. Even though my jacket is warm, I shiver. Even though it's quiet out, my head is all noise.

Even though I want to hope for the best from Joni, I fully expect the worst.

And that's the saddest, maddest thing of all.

I manage to vent most of my feelings to Noah on the phone that night and try to keep the Joni situation out of my thoughts when I get to school the next day. There are only two more days until the dance, and there is lots of architecting to do before then.

We are not focusing on death; instead, we're surrounding ourselves with all the things that remain after death—words and stones and portraits and memories. The dowager's picture is the first thing we put up on the gymnasium walls. Everything else follows suit.

We avoid black. We want to enfold death in color. Kyle emerges from a supply cabinet with his arms swathed in blue drapery—his own tribute to the dowager. Instead of asking people to dress up in costume, we've asked them to wear heirlooms. I will wear my grandfather's watch and my grandmother's heart-shaped pin. In my pocket, I will carry a monogrammed handkerchief that my other grandfather took to war; alongside it will be a letter my grandmother wrote to him in those years, full of words of undying love. I like to think that as I dance, they will be in some way alive again. I will revive them with my thoughts and feelings.

We work hard for the next forty-eight hours. Amber handles the sound, weaving excerpts from grave books and Emily Dickinson into the tunes she's chosen. We are mirrored in other people's reflections.

Ted drops by to help. I catch him flirting with Trilby as they throw streamers over the rafters. Infinite Darlene clucks her tongue from afar, but doesn't say a word.

Noah helps out, too. We've enlarged his photographs to hang in the corners, a way to draw people there. He catches me when I go to put mood candles in the space under the bleachers.

"Isn't that a fire hazard?" he asks.

"Shh," I reply, moving my finger to my lips, then letting it drop.

I light the candles. The air smells like vanilla mist. Noah reaches over to touch my cheek. His thumb moves over my lips and down the side of my neck. He leans me back against the wall and kisses me. I kiss him back hard. We breathe each other in. As the sound system tests itself out and orchids are floated atop the tables, we grasp at each other and explore each other and mark the time in movements and whispers. It's only when Trilby calls out my name that we stop.

"I guess the candles work," Noah says, pulling back and straightening his untucked shirt.

"Shh," I say again, my voice full of glimmer.

"Debauchery," he concludes with a smile. One of my dictionary words.

I always secretly believe that putting together a party is more fun than actually attending. As I tell Trilby and Ted where the dancing skeletons should hang, I see how animated we've all become. Infinite Darlene is spinning tunes with Amber and Amy. Emily is unwrapping a gilt punch bowl. Kyle is taking a practice dance with the dowager's portrait. Noah is leaning against the gym wall, readying his camera for a shot. It seems a shame that we have to let other people into this world we're creating.

Then I think of Tony, and I'm ready to open the doors.

One Small Step

Saturday night arrives and I look fabulous. I am wearing a second-hand tuxedo and a pair of shoes that shine like a Gibson guitar. I have folded a flower for Noah's lapel and have affixed my grandmother's pin with pride.

My parents are stunned when they see me. I don't look like a kid anymore. I don't look like an adult, either—but I definitely look older than a kid.

"Do you want to borrow one of my harmonicas?" my father asks (he always brings one to parties, just in case the going gets slow).

"Did you brush and floss?" my mother asks.

"Are you ready to go?" Jay says. He has a date of his own to pick up.

In the car, he thanks me.

"For what?" I ask.

"For tipping me off about you and Noah," he replies. (I had mentioned it to him, as promised, before Rip found out that Noah had asked me to the dance.)

"How much are you going to win?"

"Rip's going to owe me five hundred bucks."

"Five hundred?!?" I can't believe it. "Were the odds that much against me?"

Jay shakes his head. "No. I just bet a lot on the two of you."

Now it's my turn to say thanks. He's shown his faith, in his own twisted older-brother way.

We pick up his date, Delia Myers, who looks splendid in a purple spiral creation. She shows me a bracelet that belonged to her great-grandmother. It is the shape of two wings.

I am feeling nervous when I get to Noah's house. I still haven't met his parents. I wonder if this will be the night.

I ring the doorbell. Claudia answers. She looks surprised to see me so cleaned up.

"Is Noah home?" I ask.

"Duh," she replies.

She calls up to him.

"Your parents home?"

She shakes her head glumly.

"So I guess I should ask your permission," I say.

She looks at me like I'm a Martian. "For what?"

"To take Noah out."

"You don't need my permission."

"But I'd like it."

She looks me over again.

"I guess so."

That's all she'll give me, but I figure it's a start.

Noah comes down and I give him the flower. He hands me a photograph of a flower—it's beautiful, more vibrant in color than the real thing.

"I figured it will last longer," he says, gently placing it in my pocket.

Claudia fades into another room. Noah takes my hand.

"Let's go get Tony," he says.

We are almost out the door when Claudia returns.

"One second," she says. We turn to her and she holds up a camera. "I want to get a picture of the two of you."

She poses us by the staircase. She asks us to lean into each other, for me to put my hand on his shoulder. It's something so simple and everyday—smiling before the flash, checking to see if everything's in place. But for me it's a revelation. For the first time in my life, I truly feel part of a couple. I feel that Noah and I together are one thing. Posing for his sister's camera, heading down the front walk hand in hand to my brother's car—it's not something we have to think about. It feels natural.

Jay and Delia welcome Noah to the car and drive over to the block before Tony's. We'd all planned to meet up there and walk to his house together. Kyle is already there (I'll later find out he was the first to arrive). Infinite Darlene is there wearing a Grace Kelly gown. Trilby and Ted are there; their outfits don't match, but something in their expressions does. Amber looks amazing in a cocktail dress that used to belong to her great-grandmother, from her flapper days. Laura and her girlfriend are dressed as Hepburn and Hepburn. Emily and Amy are low-key in jeans and antique sweaters.

Joni is nowhere to be seen. The time has come for us to head to Tony's, but we don't move. Those of us who know her are still waiting for her to come. Even though we don't say anything, I know that Ted is waiting and Infinite Darlene is waiting. We still don't think she would miss this. But it's looking like we're wrong. After five minutes, Kyle says we'd better go. To my surprise, he leads the way. I walk alongside him, and he shows me a ring that his aunt gave to her husband Tom. He let Kyle borrow it for the night. I thank him for showing me.

We get to the house. The cars are in the garage. Both his parents are home. Kyle steps aside so I can be the one to ring the doorbell. I am about to do it when I hear Joni's voice say, "I'm here." I turn to look at her. Chuck is at her side, looking displeased.

"Sorry I'm late," she adds.

"No worries," I say. Then I ring the bell.

Tony's mom answers. His dad is at her side.

"We've come to pick Tony up for the dance," I say.

Tony walks up behind them, dressed in his Sunday best.

"I see," his dad says, not sounding too happy. "And are you his date?"

"We're all his date," Joni answers.

Everyone steps forward. Girls and boys. Straight boys and a drag queen. My boyfriend. My ex-boyfriend. My brother. Me.

Tony angles past his parents and joins us. His tie is crooked and his suit is brown. But I've never seen him look so marvelous.

"Can I go?" he asks.

His parents stare at him. They stare at us. His mom puts her hand over her mouth. His father steps back from the doorway.

"It looks like you're going anyway," he says sternly.

"But I want you to say I can go," Tony implores, his voice cracking.

His father looks torn between dogma and helplessness. As a result, he simply walks away.

Tony turns to his mom. Tears drop from her eyes. She looks at Infinite Darlene. She looks at Joni. She looks at me and Kyle. Then she looks at her son.

"Please," he whispers.

She nods. "Have fun," she says. "Be back by midnight."

Tony beams with relief. His mother does not, not even when he leans over to kiss her good-bye.

"Thank you," he says.

She holds him for a moment, looks into his eyes. Then she lets him go with us into the night. We all want to cheer, but we know we have to wait to do that. We've been given another reason to dance.

We head back to the cars. Tony holds back for a moment.

"Wait a second," he says.

"What?" I ask him. Everyone stops to listen.

"Can we be late for the dance?" he says. "I have an idea. . . ."

What I Will Always Remember

9 P.M. on a November Saturday. We are in a clearing surrounded by trees and bushes, under the protection of a hill we like to call a mountain. Word has spread, and most of our friends are here. The Dowager is waiting in the gym. She'll get her chance soon enough.

Someone's brought a radio, and we're dancing as the tunes dangle in the air. We are illuminated by flashlights and candles. We carry our grandfathers' cigarette cases and our grandmothers' bangles. We are young and the night is young. We are in the middle of somewhere and we are feeling everything.

The dirt is our dance floor. The stars are our elaborate decoration. We dance with abandon—only the happiness exists for us here. I spin Amber around in a tango, both of us making up the steps as we go along. Tony and Kyle are dancing next to us. Happy. Laughing.

In this space, in this moment, we are who we want to be. I am lucky, because for me that doesn't take that much courage. But for others, it takes a world of bravery to make it to the clearing.

I dance with Noah. Slow songs and fast songs. During the slow songs, more of the unsaid things are understood. *Be careful. I'm still learning. You are so beautiful. This is so beautiful.* During the fast songs, all those thoughts disappear, and there's the giddy exhilaration of being a part of the crowd, a part of the music, a part of all our differences and all the things we share.

At the next song switch, I hang back. I want to see this as well as be a part of it. I want to remember it for what it is. I am amazed by the love I feel for so many people. I am amazed at the randomness, the comedy, and the faith that brings us all together and makes us hold on. I open myself wide to take it all in. The scene plays out like a rhapsody.

I see trees of green and dresses of white. I see Infinite Darlene whooping for joy as Amber attempts to dip her to the ground. I see Ted cheering them on as he strums an air guitar. I see Kyle and Tony talking quietly together, sharing their words. I see Joni leading Chuck in a slow dance. I see candles in the darkness and a bird against the sky. I see Noah walking over to me, care in his eyes, a blessed smile on his lips.

And I think to myself, *What a wonderful world.*

About the Author

David Levithan was not born in France, Milwaukee, or Olympia, Washington. He did not go to Eton, Harvard Law School, or Oxford University. He is not the author of *War and Peace, Hollywood Wives: The New Generation,* or *Baby-sitters Club #8: Boy-crazy Stacey.* He has not won the Newbery Medal, the Pulitzer Prize, the Bausch & Lomb Science Award, or the race for eleventh-grade vice president.

He currently does not live in Manhattan.

If you doubt any of this, check www.davidlevithan.com.